The Cowboy and His Sweetheart

Rock Springs, Texas Book 4

Kaci M. Rose

Five Little Roses Publishing

Book Cover By: **Sarah Kil Creative Studio**

Editing By: Anna @ Indie Hub

Blurb

I shouldn't want him. He's older than me, he's a rough bar owning cowboy, dangerous.

But every time I'm near him I've never felt safer.

I've always been a good girl, following my parent's rules, church every Sunday, and good grades in school.

But when Jason walks into my life I'm willing to break every rule for him, only he won't let me.

This bad boy cowboy is conforming to my parent's rules proving he's worthy of me.

Until one of the guys at church start getting a little too pushy, trying to lay claim on me, stalking me, and spreading lies around the church.

Until this guy goes too far and I see a side of Jason I've never seen before, a side that could ruin everything.

Slide into the saddle and gallop into this sizzlin' cowboy romance set in the kind of small town that treasures porch swings and sweet tea!

Dedication

To the coffee that kept me going and the kids that call me Mommy.

Contents

Get Free Books!

Would you like some free cowboy books?
If you join Kaci M. Rose's Newsletter you get books and bonus epilogues free!
Join Kaci M. Rose's newsletter and get your free books!
https://www.kacirose.com/KMR-Newsletter

Now on to the story!

Chapter 1

Jason

I'm watching Sage and Colt dance, and the love on their face for each other is enough to make my heart clench; there's just no hiding it. I won't admit it to my family, but I want that too. As the oldest, I'm watching my younger siblings fall in love, and I'm so happy for them, but it makes the clock tick a little louder.

It's not that I don't want to find love; I do. Because I own the bar in town, people have preconceived notions on who I must be. I'm not some rough and tough cowboy who sleeps around.

This is the second wedding in two months. And there will be another wedding for Megan and Hunter coming up. That's three weddings in a year. Mac, my youngest brother, and I are the old holdouts now, as everyone likes to joke.

I look around the wedding reception and notice a lot of people I don't know. Sage has invited all her friends she met when she was traveling.

In the back corner, I see a table with one of those groups. It looks like a mother and father with a few kids around Sage's age. They're talking and seem to be having a good time.

Then I see her. Long blond hair and the sweetest smile as she laughs at something someone at the table says. I'm drawn to her in a way I can't explain. Then, as if she feels my eyes on her, she turns to look at me. Her eyes meet mine, and I'm a goner.

I know what the guys have been talking about. One look and I know this girl is mine. My heart is attached to hers, pulling me toward her. I take a deep breath, stand, and make my way to her table, never taking my eyes off her. When she realizes I'm heading her way, her eyes widen, causing me to smile.

I reach the table, and everyone looks at me.

"Hello, I'm Jason, Sage's brother. I just wanted to introduce myself," I say, looking at my angel.

"Well, hello, Jason!" The older man with just a bit of grey hair at his temples greets me while standing up to shake my hand. "I remember Sage talking about you. Please sit and join us."

I take the seat next to my angel and smile at her. She now looks shy, and I hate to take my eyes away from her, but I want to know who these people are she's with.

"My name is Grant Stevenson, and this is my wife Maria. These are our kids." He continues, "This is Royce my oldest, Maggie, and my youngest Ella."

Ella.

My angel's name is Ella.

I smile at everyone but turn my eyes to Ella. She looks too young for me. I'm not old but at twenty-eight, I'd bet I'm almost ten years older than.

Crap, is she even legal?

"Can I get you a drink, sweetheart?" I ask her.

She smirks. "Don't laugh, but Sage introduced me to a Shirley Temple, and I think I'm addicted."

I smile. "You should try a Mai Tai if you like those."

"Oh, nothing with alcohol."

I frown. "Not old enough to drink?"

"That's not it. I'm twenty-one. We don't believe in drinking alcohol." The look on her face says she knows my reason for asking.

Then it hits me. She doesn't believe in drinking alcohol, and I own a bar.

Lovely.

"Well, I'm going to get your Shirley Temple. When I get back, maybe you'll explain that a bit more?"

She nods and smiles. "Okay."

I make my way to the bar at the other end of the large event barn where Sage's wedding reception is being held. I get to the bar and order my drinks when I feel a hand on my shoulder. When I look over, it's Sage.

"Hey, I saw you talking to Maggie's family."

"Yeah, what can you tell me about them?"

"Oh, they're very conservative, and I know Maggie wants to stay in the same town as her family."

"Not Maggie, Ella."

"Ella caught your eye?"

I can't help the smile that covers my face. "Yeah."

"She's... young."

I sigh. "I know, but it's only seven years."

Sage looks at me like she's reading me.

"I want you happy, Jason, so you know I'm on your side, but they aren't like us. They don't date."

"What do you mean?"

"They're religious, small-town people. Great people, but they don't date. They do courtships, where you have chaperones on the dates. They don't believe in sex before marriage. Hell, they have their first kiss on their wedding day."

I look at my Ella from across the room. To think no man has ever kissed her lips is almost more than I can take.

I look back at Sage, and her face is full of concern.

"Jason, you own a bar which is everything they don't approve of. They don't dance, or drink. The girls wear dresses or skirts only, no pants. They're the kindest, sweetest people, but they're going to be so protective of her."

"Well, I guess you need to put in a good word for me. She's it, Sage. I can't change that."

She sighs. "You have one hell of an uphill battle ahead of you, big brother."

"Guess it's a good thing I love the climb."

"Just ask for her phone number. When you text, it will be a group text with her and her mom and dad. Phone calls will have someone else on the line too."

I hug Sage. "Thank you, and in case I haven't told you, you look stunning today."

"Thanks, and you have, but you can't ever compliment a bride too much!"

I pick up our drinks and head back to the table. Grant gives me a knowing smirk but once Ella catches my eye, I don't notice anyone else.

"So tell me more about this no drinking," I say to get the conversation going.

"Oh, it's just our religion. We don't believe in drinking alcohol, dancing, sex before marriage, that kind of thing. We dress modestly and treat people the way Jesus would."

I nod. "Tell me you at least drink coffee?"

She laughs. "Oh yes, I live on coffee."

"Good, me too. Where are you from?"

"Mountain Gap, Tennessee. It's a small town in the middle Tennessee."

I spend the next several hours sitting and talking with her family. I can't learn enough of my Ella, so when her father gets up to get some more water for his wife, I want to talk to him.

"Grant, hang on." I turn to Ella. "Sweetheart, you want another Shirley Temple?"

The smile that fills her face is my reward. "Yes, please!"

"Okay, I'll be right back."

I walk up to the bar with her father, and I like that he cuts right to the chase.

"I'm guessing you aren't here for my sparkling personality." He smiles.

I laugh. "No, I'd like to get to know Ella better. She mentioned you're around another few days since Sage isn't leaving for her honeymoon right away?"

"We are," he says but gives nothing away.

"I'd like to invite Ella out for a tour of the ranch. Maybe horseback riding if she's interested. I'd be honored if you would join us," I say, remembering what Sage said about them always having chaperones.

"You know we don't date?"

"Yes, Sage told me a bit about courtship. I'm not asking for anything other than to spend the day getting to know her a bit more. Letting you and her get to know me."

"How old are you, Jason?"

"Twenty-eight, sir."

I must look nervous because he smiles. "My Maria is six years younger than me. I met her when I was your age. Ella is a lot like her mother."

He nods and looks back at the table.

"Sage is an amazing person. She and Maggie became good friends, and I'm sure Royce was crushing on her for a bit, but she was always upfront that her heart was Colt's. I respect that. You're from the same stock so for that reason, I'm not saying no, outright. Sell yourself to me. Who are you, Jason? Make it good; this might be your one chance."

Damn, this guy is good. I'm glad Ella has someone so loving watching out for her and protecting her, but I don't see him being okay with a bar owner wanting to get to know his daughter.

Taking a deep breath, I decide to go for honestly. "I'm the oldest of the family and get so much ribbing because three of them are now married, and another is engaged. They can't even get me on a date. I've had two serious girlfriends, one in high school and one when I was about twenty-one. She broke up with me when Waylon died, and I inherited the bar."

I watch him open his mouth. "Let me finish please." He eyes me then nods.

"Right after that, one of the girls in town was drugged. It was my sign to clean things up. So I did a remodel. I brought in a great friend of mine who I went to school with to be the chef, and we turned it into a restaurant. He just won a BBQ award recently. I put in a stage, and we have live music on Friday and Saturday nights. I was just approached to consider becoming a small concert venue stop on a country music tour. One show a month, and we are in negotiations for that. It stands to bring some good revenue to the town. I love this ranch and the land, but it was never my dream to run it. That's Blaze and Sage, and now Colt. It wasn't my dream to own the bar either, but it's not really a bar anymore. It's a family friendly place in town to eat and hear some good local music."

I pause for a breath. "I'm telling you this because I want to be honest. I'm hardworking, love my family with all that I have. I don't go to church every Sunday, but Mom gets me there more often than not. I know I'm probably the opposite of what you want for your daughter but when I saw her tonight from across the room, I just knew I had to meet her and that she would be in my life. I can't explain it, but I can't just walk away. Not unless she makes me. I have nothing to hide, and I just want you, your family, and her to get to know me."

I feel like I've talked in circles and said too much but at the same time, not enough. He looks deep in thought, and his reaction could go either way. If he were to say no, I'm not sure what I would do. I don't think I could stay away from her.

"Well, why don't we see if she wants a tour of the ranch tomorrow. Normally, I'd say no, but I know Sage is good people. I love my girls, but it's their choice, their life. I'm just here to weed out the bad guys, the ones without good intentions. I look forward to getting to know you more, Jason. But to be clear, this isn't a yes. This is let's get to know each other." He shakes my hand, and we grab our drinks and head back. I feel a bit of relief as part of the hill has been tackled.

I set Ella's drink in front of her and sit back down.

"Thank you." She smiles. "What were you talking to Dad about?"

"You." Her face falls, but I smile. "I'd like to give you a tour of the ranch tomorrow. Sage has been talking about starting a garden, and you mentioned you love gardening. I'd like your thoughts on where to place it, and how to get started. I thought maybe we could go for a ride on the horses. I also invited your dad to join us."

She looks over at her dad, and he nods. "It's up to you, Ella bug."

She looks over at her mom, then her brother and sister. My heart races and my mouth is dry as I wait for her answer. She takes so long I start to second guess myself. Maybe she isn't interested like I thought. Maybe she is just being nice to the creepy older guy sitting next to her.

Then she looks back at me. "I'd love to, Jason. Sage has asked us to come up to the main house for breakfast. Will I see you then?"

I let out a huge breath I didn't know I had been holding "Yes, I'll be there." I can't help the huge smile that has taken over my face.

"Well, I think we'll call it a night, but maybe you can help us, so we don't have to bug Sage. We got in today and haven't even been shown where we're staying. She said the main house," Grant says.

"Yes, Jason can show you," Sage says from my left. I hadn't heard her come up. "Jason, her parents are staying in the guest master. Royce is in the midnight room, and Maggie and Ella are down the hall in the garden rooms. You'll each have your own space, but the girls will share a Jack and Jill bath."

Sage says goodbye to everyone, and we head out of the barn. The night air is cooler than inside the barn, and the sky is clear. Ella walks beside me and looks up at the sky.

"It's so clear out here, it makes the sky look so big." She's still looking up when she trips over a rock on the side of the path.

I reach out and catch her, pulling her against me to stop her from falling. Having her body pressed to mine, it's like time stopped. Her eyes meet mine, and mine are locked on her. My heart races. When my mind works again, I set her back on her feet and step away, putting space between us.

I watch her look down, and her face turns red, "Sorry," she mumbles.

"No need to be sorry, sweetheart. I'll always catch you. Let's head to the main house. The sky is amazing from the front yard there."

She smiles, and I feel like I've just won the lottery. Knowing I made her smile is the best feeling in the world. I get in my truck, and she and her family follow in their van. We must go back out almost to the main gate and swing back down to the driveway to the main house, and I smile the whole way.

Chapter 2

Ella

I watch the main house come into view, and it's just beautiful. It looks more like a mansion than a farmhouse, but Jason is right. The front yard is wide open, perfect for stargazing. When Dad parks the van, Jason is right there, opening the door for me.

He's nothing like I thought he would be when Sage would talk about him. All night, all I wanted was to keep him talking to hear more and learn more about him. He's interested in what I have to say too.

Then on the way out, when I tripped, and he caught me, his skin on mine was electric I can still feel his chest pressed against mine. I know now why my parents have a limited touch rule until marriage. If I feel like that when we touch, I know I'll want to be that close to him all the time.

"Look, you can see the sky well from here," Jason says, pointing up.

"I wish I knew more about constellations. I bet you can see many of them from here."

My Dad, brother, and Jason grab our bags, and we head inside. We walk in the side door into a kitchen dining room area. Beyond that is a massive living room.

"Sage lives here?" I ask as I take it all in. I'm pretty sure this downstairs is bigger than our whole house!

"Well, we all do," he says and looks a bit shy.

"What?" I ask.

"This was Sage's family's home, and she had it remodeled. She asked all of us kids to move in, so we live in the family wing. Sage and Colt will have the master. Blaze and Riley, and Megan and Hunter have already said they'd stay here until they have kids. Riley is pregnant, so they're remodeling one of the family cabins and will move in there when it's done, but that's still a year or so away. Mac and I have our own rooms too."

We head upstairs, and Jason stops at the landing, and my family stops behind us.

He points to the right. "Down there's the family wing. In front of us and to the left are the guest rooms." He points to a room in front of him to the left. "This is your room, Royce, the midnight room."

Royce nods and heads in with his bag. Jason turns down to the left, and we head down the hall. He stops at the end and looks at my parents.

"Sage has you two in the master here. You girls can pick from either of those rooms. We call them the garden rooms; one is done in roses, and the other in sunflowers.

I follow Dad into the sunflower room and take it in as he sets down my bag. Pale-yellow walls, light-wood floor, all white furniture, and a soft pale-yellow comforter on the bed. A farmhouse décor and several photos of sunflowers. The dresser has sunflower pulls to it as well.

"I love this room; it's bright and modern but cozy too."

"That's all Sage. She had so many home design magazines when we were working on this house. She planned every room," Jason says.

Dad goes to the far end of the room and takes in the view from the window. I walk over to Jason who is standing in the doorway and has entered the room.

"I really enjoyed talking with you tonight," I say with a shy smile.

"I did too. Is it too early to ask for your phone number, so we can chat?"

"No, let me get my phone."

Dad turns around. "All texts must be via group chat with her mother and myself. Calls must be planned and chaperoned until we're more comfortable with you. We monitor her phone."

"I understand, and I wouldn't expect anything else."

We exchange numbers, and Jason heads off to bed. I'm lying in bed replaying the whole night when my phone goes off.

I see it's Jason, and he follows the rules by including Mom and Dad.

Jason: I had a really good time tonight. Good night, Ella. I'll see you at breakfast.

Me: I had a good time too. See you at breakfast.

Dad: Good night, kids.

I have to laugh. That's Dad's way of saying it's too late. Jason takes the hint as well, and I fall asleep with a smile on my face.

• • • • • • • • • •

I wake up the next morning to the smell of bacon and coffee. Remembering where I am and that I'm meeting Jason for breakfast and a day on the ranch gets me out of bed.

I decide to dress country and wear a black and red plaid shirt dress with black leggings under it, so I'm ready for whatever the day brings. I top it off with a thin brown belt to give the dress shape and my brown cowgirl boots. I leave my long blond hair down and give it a little curl, swipe on some mascara, and I'm off.

I head downstairs and find Royce already there, along with a couple I don't recognize as well as Sage, Colt, and Jason in the kitchen.

"Good morning, sweetheart," Jason says when he sees me. I love that he calls me that.

"Oh my God, I love your outfit!" Sage says. "You always have the best style. I need to go shopping with you again soon. I miss that."

"Anytime," I say.

"Hi, I'm Megan, and this is my fiancé Hunter," the girl I don't recognize says. She's still in her pajama pants and a t-shirt with her brown hair pulled up in a messy bun. Hunter has that classic blond hair, blues eyes, and muscular build. He smiles and nods my way, but he barely takes his eyes off Megan.

Everyone seems to pile into the kitchen after that, and the whole house buzzes as everyone piles their plates. I'm trying to figure out where to sit when Jason comes up beside me.

"Here, let's sit at the kitchen island. Is that okay?" he asks. It's right next to the dining room table, so I nod. Over breakfast, we talk about food, what we like and what we don't. We talk about music and animals. I find out that Hunter is a vet and runs the animal clinic in town with his dad. His dad works in the office, and he does the house calls.

After breakfast, Dad comes up to us. "So, what's on the agenda?" he asks Jason.

"Well, I thought we could walk the grounds here and show you around. There's a spot we were looking at for a garden near the family graveyard back on my parents' side. Then we could end up here for lunch and go horseback riding this afternoon to see more of the property. Be back for dinner?"

"Sounds perfect," I say, and he smiles at me.

Dad nods. "Okay, let's go."

"If you see something you want to check out, just let me know," he says. "I thought we'd start in the barn here. This is where Sage keeps the horses she's training."

We walk in the barn. It's huge, as long as a football field easily. The front looks a lot like a stable where the back resembles what I would expect an animal barn to look like.

"Sage is training all these horses?" I ask. There must be almost twenty of them.

"No, some are ranch horses, some are here for breeding. Riley was helping with the training until she got pregnant. Now, Blaze won't let her; he's crazy protective."

He talks a bit about some of the horses and how they sort cattle in the different fields as we walk to his parents' side of the ranch.

"Why is the ranch split like this?" Dad asks.

"Well, my parents' side, the east side, was the first part. Sage's side, the west side, was her family's land. To spare you the details, her dad was an abusive drunk, and Mom and Dad adopted her at age twelve. She saw them ignore the land after she left and said she wanted to buy it. So, we came up with the plan and Dad opened a savings account. We all worked to save money. That's how Sage got into horse training. I took a job cleaning the bar after school before they opened. Later, I bartended before I started managing it. We all stayed at home and saved as much money as possible. When we bought it, we merged it into all one ranch but to even the load, we run it this way. Blaze and Mac run the east side, Sage and Colt run the west side, and we all help where needed."

We make our way behind his parents' house and up a footpath to a graveyard.

"This is the family graveyard. My whole family has been buried here, starting with my great-great-grandparents who settled the land here."

The graveyard has a stone border and wrought-iron fence and gate around it. Some massive trees give it shade, and it looks very peaceful and well kept.

"Sage was looking over here for a garden. What do you think?" He walks over to a huge empty area to the side of the graveyard.

"The ground looks good, but the trees would throw off some shade. You want it in a wide-open area, with nothing to block the sun."

I'm enjoying my time with him, and I'm dreading having to leave tomorrow. I've been wondering all day if this can go anywhere. Will my parents allow it because he isn't from our church? They always made comments about finding a nice church boy for Maggie.

After lunch, we head out horseback riding, and I love it. He seems to be more himself on the horse; he laughs more and is more relaxed. I feel more relaxed too, and Dad is getting along well with him. I hope this is a good sign.

Chapter 3

Jason

Ella and her family left this morning. It was the hardest thing to say goodbye when I had no idea when or if I'd get to see her again. All I know is I need to make it happen. We agreed to keep texting and getting to know each other, and we promised to be completely open and honest to each other, nothing off limits.

I'm sitting down with Mac, Blaze, Riley, Colt, and Sage now in the living room. I need a game plan. Blaze and Riley are already here. I'm watching Riley rub her barely there baby bump as she sits on Blaze's lap. He has one arm around her waist and his hand over her belly like he's protecting the baby.

That's Blaze, he protects those he loves, and he's extra protective of Riley. Don't judge him too hard though; it was hard to see Riley thrown across the room like a rag doll when her ex-boyfriend broke into the house. Blaze shot the guy dead, and if he didn't do it, I'm sure Colt would have after the guy sliced Sage's chest deep with a hunting knife.

Those times are behind us, and everyone is happier now. Sage and Colt enter the room, followed by Mac. Colt sits on the couch, and Sage snuggles up next to him, watching Blaze and Riley with a smile on her face.

"What's up, big brother?" Sage finally asks.

I lean forward, putting my elbows on my knees, and rub my hands together. I just need to be honest about it. Just man up, these guys will get it.

"Ella is the one."

That's all I have to say, and all five of them cheer, excited for me. I can't stop smiling.

"I need your help, guys. You know how her family is. We're going to take some time and text, but watching her leave today tore my heart out. I wanted to chase after her and say to hell with everything here."

"I know that feeling very well," Colt says. Sage up and left many years ago, and he had to fight the urge to chase her too. Sage looks at him, leans in to kiss his cheek, and whispers in his head. He closes his eyes and rests his cheek on the top of her head.

"I want to visit her, but I don't know what to do with the bar."

"Well, I can help while you're gone, and so can Nick," Colt says. Nick is a good friend and the chef at the bar; he runs the place on nights I'm not there.

"I can go in and help too. You know I'm not letting Colt go to the bar alone," Sage says. We all laugh. We know Kelli likes to frequent the bar. She's the girl who isn't Colt's ex but the closest he has to it, and she caused all sorts of problems between Sage and Colt.

"I can help make dinner when you guys are at the bar. I've been finishing my schoolwork before lunch each day," Riley says.

"And I can take over anything on this side of the ranch," Mac adds.

"Okay, now that we have that out of the way, Sage, I'm flying blind here. Her dad agreed to let us talk but now what?"

"You have to take it slow. I know that's not a trait with you men when you finally fall, but you have to. Let them get to know you over the next month before you visit. When you're there, talk to her dad about courting her. That's where you get the title boyfriend and girlfriend. You have to court for a few months. This is where you talk about marriage and how you would raise a family, to see if a life together is possible. From there, you have to talk to her dad before proposing. The good news is once engaged, they move fast to get married."

"How fast?" Riley asks.

"Maggie's friend was married in twenty-eight days. It's their culture. But once married, the husband and wife set the standards for their marriage. I've seen some girls get married and wear jeans. One got a nose ring. They aren't prudes; they just honor their parents' wishes until they're married."

"And they don't have their first kiss until their wedding day?" Riley asks again.

"Yeah, each couple sets their standards. Holding hands is a big thing; it mostly happens at engagement. Side hugs during courting. Always chaperoned when together; they're never alone."

Sage and Riley keep talking about her time spent with them, but all I can think about is Ella. She has been gone for about three hours, and I miss her like crazy.

Me: Hey, just wanted to check how your drive is going.

Ella: Just stopped at the Arkansas welcome center.

Me: State you want to see most and why?

Ella: Wyoming. Grand Teton National Park and Yellowstone are right next to each other and so different! You?

Me: Maine. The rocky coast and Acadia. I want to sit on top of Cadillac Mountain and be one of the first in the country to see the sun come up.

That's how it goes all day, a game of twenty questions getting to know each other on a basic level. Hobbies, food, movies, music, colors, people, pet peeves. We cover it all before she gets home.

• • • ♦ ● • ♦ ♦ • •

It's been a week since Ella left and when I'm not texting her, I'm working my butt off, so I have less time to miss her. In theory anyway. I still miss her like crazy.

In one conversation, I mention how busy the bar is since adding on the food, and she suggests outdoor seating since it would be more family friendly for those coming in just for the food. She says fans and heaters could be added so it can be used all year if there's a cover like a tent. So I've been looking into that. She has been sending me pictures of Pinterest and even made a board of ideas.

Megan had to explain Pinterest to me, but the ideas Ella has are amazing.

I'm doing inventory at the bar when a man in a suit walks in. I can tell he's not from here. He screams city all over him, and not Dallas city but New York City kind of city.

"Hello, I'm looking for Jason Buchanan?" he asks as he walks up to me at the bar.

"That would be me."

"Hello Jason, I'm Dean Greenwall I'm a producer for the Food TV show BBQ Champions. I wanted to talk to you about being on the show. Do you have a moment?"

"Why us?"

"Well, it's my understanding your chef recently won a BBQ award in Dallas?"

"Yes."

"That's what the show is about. We follow the winners back to where they cook and talk about their win, their food, how they come up with the recipes. It would give exposure to him but also your establishment."

"Nick!" I call toward the kitchen.

"Yeah, boss."

"This gentleman wants to feature you and WJ's on a TV show. You interested in hearing what he has to say?"

I watch Nick's eyes light up, and that's all I need to know.

"Let's grab a table, and we can hear him out."

Dean gives us the rundown of how they come in before the place opens to do footage. Then they shoot some in the kitchen while he's cooking before it gets busy. Then he talks about how they're here one evening as well, so they have plenty of what he calls 'B-roll' footage.

"Well, will you give us a few days to talk it over?" I ask.

"Of course! Here's my card with my cell on it. Call or text even if you have a question. There's a YouTube channel with our past shows, so you can get a feel for it as well."

We watch him leave, then Nick looks at me "This would bring in a lot of business, wouldn't it?"

"Yeah, it would. I was thinking of adding an outdoor seating area for families. It would expand seating too. We'll need it if we do the show; the business has picked up just on you winning the award."

"That your idea?"

I smile. "Actually, it was Ella's."

Nick smiles. "She's good for you. I notice a difference with you the last week, and it's good. Listen, I'm all for doing the show but go home. Talk to your family; it will affect them too. It could be good for the town as well. Maybe consider opening for lunch once the show airs. People come for the day, go shopping on Main, and have some food. Who knows?"

"Thanks, I'm going to step out and make some phone calls."

Nick pats me on the shoulder then heads back to the kitchen. I head out to my truck and text Ella.

Me: Is there someone with you, so I can call you. I have some news!

Ella: Let me get Mom. Hang on. Good news?

Me: Yes.

I'm excited by my news, but this is also the first phone call I'll have with my angel. It's been a week since I heard her voice, and now I'm nervous and excited at the same time.

Ella: Ready when you are.

I take a deep breath and call her.

"Hey," she says softly.

"Hey, sweetheart. How's your day been?"

"Good so far. You're on speaker, and Mom is here. Dad might come in once he sees the texts."

"That's good. So, I was at the bar doing inventory, and a guy in a suit walks in. He was from the BBQ Champions show. Have you heard of it?"

"Yes! We love that show."

"Well, they want to do an episode on us since Nick won that award."

I go on to tell her what he said.

"Jason, that sounds amazing. It's a good show, very family friendly, and would be great exposure for your place and for Nick."

"Yeah, that's what Nick said too. He suggested once it airs we try opening for lunch with the outdoor seating you suggested, so people can come from Dallas for the day, have lunch, hit the shops and all."

"Yes, it would open it more to families who don't want to drive home after dinner."

We talk for another twenty minutes about how her day is going and the work she's doing in the garden.

"Hey, sweetheart, I could stay on and talk to you all day, but I need to call Sage and get her to have everyone at dinner tonight, so we can talk about this."

"You haven't told them yet?"

"No, I called you first."

She's quiet for a minute, and I worry I scared her off.

"Is that okay?" I ask.

"Jason, it's more than okay. I like that I was the first one you thought to call." I can hear the smile in her voice.

"Okay, keep texting me, and we'll talk again soon?"

When we hang up, I call Sage, and she promises to get everyone to dinner tonight. Just as I hang up with Sage, a text comes in.

Ella: Can you send pictures of the WJ's? I'd like to see it.

I smile and take some photos outside, showing her where I think her outdoor setting idea would work, and then head in to get some of the dance floor, bandstand, and some of my beer can American flag on the wall behind the bar. It's a showstopper, and one of the things we're known for in the area.

I take some of the walls; they have old barn wood on them from local barns in the area, and each section has the barn and family's name it came from. Then there are ranch brands from all the local ranches seared into the wood on the walls too.

She asks about my family's brand, and I say yes, it's by the bar, and send her a picture. We chat a bit about the design for the outdoor seating, and I mention I know a designer from the reservation who might want to help. That leads to a conversation about our family's relationship with the reservation and how we've helped each other for generations.

She's interested in everything about the ranch, WJ's, and the family, and I love being able to share it all with her.

Chapter 4

Ella

It's been a week since my phone call with Jason. This day is dragging. I have another phone call set with him tonight. I'm out in the garden pulling what few weeds there are. I've been out here a lot lately, trying to keep busy. It's always been what has calmed my nerves.

I hear the gate squeak open, and I glance over my shoulder and see Dad.

"Hey, Ella Bug."

"Hey, Dad," I say but don't get up. He'll tell me not to anyway.

"You've spent a lot of time in here lately."

"Yeah, lots on my mind."

"That doesn't have to do with a certain cowboy in Texas, does it?"

"It has everything to do with him."

"I figured. I also haven't seen this garden look this good since your momma and I were courting. You know she would come out here just like this when she was thinking about me. Of course, her parents and my parents were together all the time, so she was here a lot."

I've heard this story a lot about how they grew up together and hadn't thought of courting each other until their families suggested it. Then they both spent months stewing on it until Dad said they should give it a try. If it didn't work out, no hard feelings. Well, it did work out. Here they are almost thirty years later.

"If he's on your mind this much, there's a reason," my father says.

"I miss him, Daddy. I hate the distance between us. I hate how little we get to talk on the phone because of schedules, and I hate this churning in my gut I get every time I think about what you or the church would say when I tell you he's it for me, Daddy. I feel it in my bones."

I'm staring at the tomato plant in front of me and not at my father, but I hear his sharp intake of breath. I can almost hear the wheels in his head ticking.

"I won't lie. I never pictured you with a bar owner, and if hadn't been Sage's brother, I would have been guilty of pre-judging him and saying no before he even got a chance to talk to you. I've had a lot of time to think as you two have been talking. I don't think the church's opinion matters much here, so you let me deal with them. Bug, your momma and I agreed early on that we would never force our kids to marry or force you to stay in this life if you weren't happy. You're free to marry *anyone* you want. I'll always give my opinion. I just want you to think long and hard about what life you want to have with your husband, whoever it might be. How do you want to raise your kids? He owns a bar, but we don't drink, which opens a whole new lifestyle you need to consider. Do I want you in a bar? No."

I stand, dust myself off, and look him in the eye as he continues, "If you're okay with him owning a bar, then so be it. If you decide to wear jeans and drink wine once you're married, we'll support it if you're happy. The rules you follow now are ours for while you live in our house. Once you move on, they can be whatever you decide."

I have tears in my eyes, so I reach up and hug him. I see many girls at church forced into courtships they want nothing to do with, so to have this choice means everything to me.

"What do you think of him, Daddy, truly think of him?"

"If I take away the fact he owns a bar, I think he's a very respectful young man. He didn't grow up in our culture, but he has respected it, you, and our wishes. To me, that shows how much he cares about you. He's a hard worker, building up that bar from what it used to be, and he cares for his family, which is the sign of a good man. I think it's still a little early, and I'd like to see you two get to know each other more, but I think tonight when you take his phone call, you don't have to put it on speakerphone. Just stay in a public area of the house. I think we'll allow you more phone time. Text messages need to stay in the group though."

I'm so excited I let out a squeal and jump up and down before I hug him again.

"Thank you, Daddy! I love you!"

"I love you too, Ella Bug. Let's head in for dinner before they eat without us."

After dinner, I'm sitting in the living room, waiting for his call. Dad is in his office and Mom is in the kitchen where she can see and hear me.

Jason: Now a good time?
Me: Yes

I barely hit send, and my phone is ringing. I take a deep breath and answer it.

"Hello," I answer.

"Hello sweetheart, everything okay? You sound different."

"Yes." I can't help the smile on my face. "I talked with Dad today about you, and he agreed to no more group calls. We can talk whenever, just you and me. I just have to be in the public areas of the house with someone around, and texts still have to stay in the group."

"Ella, angel, that's such good news."

"I miss you, Jason," I say, lowering my voice.

"I miss you too, angel," he groans.

"I want to run something by you before I talk to your dad."

"Okay?"

"Well, I was talking to my family, and we all agreed to do the TV show. They want to film in ten days. Sage and Colt offered to take over the bar for a week. After that, I was thinking of coming up to visit you for a week, if you're okay with that."

"Really?!" I squeal.

It makes him laugh, and I get a questioning look from Mom.

"Yes, really. I take that as a yes?"

"Yes!"

"Okay. Is your dad there? I'd like to talk to him about it and nail things down now."

"Let me find him. I think he's in his office." Mom nods, so I head in there.

"Hey, Daddy? Jason wants to talk to you." I hand him the phone.

"I'll be in the kitchen with Mom," I tell him.

I head out and fill Mom in on what Jason said. A few minutes later, Dad calls me back into his office and hands me the phone, giving me a wink.

"Hello?" I ask, not sure if he's still on the line.

"Hey, sweetheart. I got the dates and details nailed down with your dad. It looks like I'll be seeing you in two weeks. This will be my first time away from the bar ever. The thought has always made me nervous before but now? I can't wait to get away from it because it means I'll be seeing you."

"Jason, I'm so excited!"

He laughs. "Good, me too. Tell me what you did with your day today."

"I spent it mostly in the garden, thinking about you. I might have to expand the garden just for something to do."

"If you could do anything, no worrying about what you should do, what anyone wants you to do, or money, what would you do?"

"Honestly, I love doing my sister's hair, and I always get asked to do the girls' hair for weddings at church."

"Have you thought of going to school for it?"

"Yeah, but I don't know where I'd work when I'm done. There aren't many salons here."

"Well, my sister Megan owns the salon here in town, and she's looking for another girl. One of the girls is just there temporarily. In about four to six months, she'll have an open chair."

I don't know what to say. Is he hinting about a job, about me moving there? It's like he can read my mind.

"I don't want to scare you but yeah, that's where my mind is, Ella. I want you here with me. When I picture my future, you're it. If I thought you and your daddy would say yes, I'd ask to start courting you today and ask for your hand in marriage tomorrow. But I'll take my time and do it right, as long as I end up with you in the end."

"Jason," I whisper, not sure what to say.

"Just think about it, okay?"

I take a deep breath. "Okay."

We spend the next half hour talking before he has to go.

"Can I talk to you tomorrow?" he asks.

"I have an event at church tomorrow. I should be out sometime after lunch."

"Well, how about you call me whenever you can? Don't worry about the time. I just want to hear your voice."

I agree, and we hang up.

· · · ● · ● ● · · ·

I'm at church the next day at a welcome event for the new members who have joined us in the last few months. My family is big on these events and always likes to welcome people to church. This time, I'm just not feeling it. I think it's because Jason is on my mind.

I'm standing off to the side of the room with a plate of some finger foods, just staring off into space, when I feel someone touch my arm. I didn't hear anyone come up, so it scares me so much, I jump.

"I'm so sorry. I thought you might have heard me walk up," a man says who I've never seen before.

"Sorry, just so lost in thought. I was in my own little world."

"Sorry, didn't mean to startle you. My name is Seth. I'm one of the newbies here and saw you standing all by yourself. I thought I'd come over and say hi."

"Oh well, welcome. My parents are floating around here. This is really their thing. They're on the committee that puts this all together." I can't place it, but something in my gut doesn't like this guy. Dad says to always trust my gut, but he's new here, so I know I have to make him feel welcome too.

"How long have you been going to church here?" he asks.

"My whole life. My parents have been members since they were kids."

"What do you think of it honestly?"

I laugh. "Well, seeing how I'm an adult, I wouldn't be here if I didn't like it." I didn't mean to snap at him, but something isn't sitting right with me.

I take a good look at him. He's not as tall as Jason, but his hair is jet black and styled almost too perfect. He's in khaki pants and a blue button-up shirt. Nothing seems out of place, but the way he looks at me sets me off. I look around, trying to find my parents, and see Dad on the other side of the event room.

I shift away from him, trying to put some space between us. He shifts towards me.

Crap on a shingle.

"So, what do you do then, miss adult?" he says with a small smile. I can't tell if what he says is skeevy, or I'm just annoyed, so everything will sound annoying. I just know I don't like it.

I take a deep breath and try to find some grace and the manners Momma taught me.

"Well, I do a lot of the girls' hair for the weddings and events here, and I work our family's garden. I work in the childcare room during services and help babysit as well."

"Wow, you sound pretty busy. A girl like you shouldn't be working so much. You should be married to a guy who's taking care of you, so you can have babies of your own."

Is this guy for real? All I can do is blink at him for a moment before my brain works again.

"Well, I enjoy what I do, so I wouldn't call it work."

"Still you should be with someone like me."

"I don't know you."

"That's what courting is for."

Is this guy serious? This has to be a joke, right? Vicky or Emma must have put him up to this. I look around, move toward the refreshment table, and make it look like I'm getting a drink, but he follows.

"I just made you a good offer. Girls would die to be with guys like me. I have enough money, so you could have anything you want and never have to worry a day in your life."

Okay, now I'm starting to panic a bit. He doesn't understand the subtle brush off. He's closing in on my space and following me across the room. I move again, toward where I last saw Dad.

"Well, I'm not interested. Excuse me, I need to find my father," I say as I walk off, but he still follows me. I'm trying not to make a scene, but I pick up my pace when I see Dad. He sees me and smiles but as soon as he sees my face, his smile falls.

I rush to him and hide behind him. I literally put him between me and Seth; so much for being an adult. I put my hand on his back, needing his comforting connection.

"Is this your father?" Seth asks and when I don't answer, Dad does.

"Yes, I'm Grant Stevenson, and who might you be?" Dad extends his hand to shake Seth's.

"I'm Seth. I'm new to the church and was talking to your daughter before she took off," he says so sweet, you would think I was in the wrong. I can't help but grip Dad's shirt. He must feel it because his whole posture changes.

"Where did you go to church before this?" Dad asks.

"Back in a small town in Indiana, no one has ever heard of. I had met the pastor here at an event, so when I was looking to set up a new office in Nashville, this place came to mind. I don't want to live in the city being a small-town boy myself."

"Well, welcome, and we'll see you around. If you'll excuse us, my daughter and I need to find my wife. We promised to help her with a few things."

"Sure thing, and ahh, I never did get your daughter's name."

Dad pauses. I can tell, just like me, he's hesitant and doesn't want to be rude.

"Well, her name is Ella, but if you need anything, you contact me."

"Sure thing. Nice to meet you, Mr. Stevenson."

I watch Seth walk off, and my father takes my hand. Without a word, he leads me toward the back hallway into one of the empty offices and closes the door. He turns to me and looks me up and down.

"What's wrong, Ella Bug?" he says so softly.

I sigh and sit in one of the chairs.

"I tried so hard to be nice, I swear I did, but you always said to trust my gut. He made me uncomfortable. Standing a little bit too close at first. I would shift away, and he would shift closer."

I go on to tell Dad what he had said and how he wouldn't leave me alone. By the time I'm done, my hands are shaking.

"Daddy, he made me so uncomfortable. I just want to go home. Please. I know this event means a lot to you and Momma..."

He interrupts me, "But you mean more. How about I get Royce to take you home? I know he can't wait to leave."

I nod, and Daddy calls my brother and waits with me until he gets here. Dad explains to Royce what happened, and I can see my brother get mad. He's very overprotective of me and my sister.

"Come on, ladybug. Let's get you home," Royce says.

I smile. He started calling me ladybug when I was obsessed with finding ladybugs when I

was six. The name stuck since Daddy calls me
Ella Bug.

He puts his arm around my shoulder as we
walk to the car. I feel safe, and relax as we head
home.

Chapter 5

Jason

I've never seen anything like the TV crew that has taken over my bar. They have lights and cameras, producers, and assistants. There's a young guy in charge of getting the history of the bar from me and asking any questions that come up, so they have their facts right. Mostly, the attention is on Nick.

I can tell he's a bit nervous. He is never one to like being in the center of attention, but he also knows this will do some great things for not just the bar and the town but his career too. He could move to Dallas and get a great job at some BBQ place and make double or even triple what he makes now, but he loves Rock Springs and by the grace of God, wants to stay here. I wouldn't blame him one bit for leaving if he ever wants to.

"Jason, can you tell me a bit about the previous owner?"

"Waylon?" I ask.

"Yes, how you met him, any history you know of him starting this place."

I smile. It's been a while since I've talked about Waylon and him starting the bar. It wasn't ever his dream. He just saw a need in town and filled it. I tell them how I was looking for work to save up money, and he gave me a job cleaning up after school, then he would kick me out when they opened. I tell them how he taught me how to bartend before I was legally allowed. So the day I turned twenty-one, I could be behind the bar and earn better tips.

I tell them about how he wanted to slow down, so he brought me on as manager and later changed the name to WJ's to include me in it. I didn't know then, but that was when he changed his will and left it to me.

They ask about when I made the changes to bring in food and hire Nick. It's hours and hours of questions and by the end, I'm thankful they're leaving. It's a Monday, and we decide to close the bar tonight. Mondays are slow, and everyone in town understands with the TV crew being here will bring a boost to the town, so they're more than happy.

Jo decides to keep the café open tonight for those who still want to go out to grab dinner. I'm sure the place is packed as people watch what goes on here and gossip all evening.

Once it's just Nick and me in the bar, I let out a sigh and pat him on the back.

"What do we need to do?"

"Not much. You know they had someone in there cleaning dishes for me? I just need to put a few things away, and I'm done."

"Okay, why don't you lock up and head to the café to feed the gossip mill."

He laughs. "Go home and get some rest. You have a long drive tomorrow."

I can't help but smile. Tomorrow, I get to see my girl. I plan to talk to her dad while I'm there about moving forward with courtship. I want to plan our life together.

· · · ● · ● · · ·

I crossed the Tennessee border about an hour ago, and the GPS says I have an hour and half of a drive left when I pull off to get gas in a little town. The first thing I do is check my phone like I have every time I stopped today.

This time I find a picture Ella sent of some double chocolate cookies she and her mom made today.

Me: Stopped for gas, and now my mouth is watering.

Ella: Mom won't even let me try one.

Me: Why?

Maria: Because if she eats one, there will be none left when you get here.

I laugh. Her mom has been joining in on our texts more and more. Ella loves it because it means her mom is warming up to the idea of us as a couple. I still have no idea where her dad stands, and I hope to find out while I'm here this week.

Me: An hour and a half longer. I just got gas, so no more stopping until I'm there.

Ella: I can't wait! Drive safe.

Me: Always.

I get back in the car and crank up the radio. Before I know it, I'm driving down the long dirt driveaway to her house. The ranch-style home comes into view, and it's a home that looks like people live here. It's comfortable with a front porch swing and rocking chairs out front. There's a clothesline off to the side, and Ella's garden is to the other side of the house.

I barely turn the car off when Ella bursts out of the front door with the largest smile on her face, and it knocks the breath out of me. I thought I remembered every detail of my angel, but seeing her now in person, I know my memories can't hold a candle to the real thing.

Ella is in a white and grey plaid shirt dress that looks a lot like the one she wore the last time I saw her on our date around the ranch. She has a thin brown belt cinching it at her waist. She has black leggings on underneath and grey boots that only go up to her ankle. Her long blond hair is down in wavy curls flowing behind her as she rushes over to me.

I see her mom and dad step onto the porch as well, and it takes everything in me not to rush over to her and sweep her up in a huge hug and hold her tight. She stops a few feet in front of me, and we both smile at each other for a minute before she steps close to give me a side hug that isn't anywhere near long enough, but I'll take what I can get.

"You're really here," she says.

"I'm really here. I thought this day would never come."

"I know what you mean."

"Good to see you, Jason." Her dad comes up and pats me on the shoulder.

"You too, sir. Mrs. Stevenson, it's good to see you as well. Please tell me they didn't eat all the cookies. They're all I've thought about since my last stop."

Maria beams a large smile at me. "I kept them away. Come inside."

I grab my bag, and her dad takes it from me. They have a guest cottage on the back of the property. He is nice enough to let me use it, so he tells me he's taking my bag out there for me.

Their house is warm and welcoming with light-wood floors and natural paint colors on the walls. I walk into a formal living room and follow her mom to the back of the house with a large kitchen, dining room, and family room combo.

The cookies are set up on the kitchen counter, and her mom offers me one. I take a bite and can't help but moan.

"Don't tell Mom, but these are even better than hers," I say, making Maria and Ella smile.

"It's the secret ingredients and doesn't ask. I won't tell you," Maria says, making everyone laugh.

"Come in and sit down. You've had a long drive," Grant says.

"No offense but if it's okay, I'd prefer to stand for a bit. I need to stretch my legs."

"Well, in that case, why don't we go for a walk outside, you and me. I'd like to chat before Ella steals all your attention."

"Dad!"

"It's okay, Ella. I stole all your mom's attention too."

I follow Ella's dad out the back door and fall in step beside him. We walk toward the back tree line of his property. I'm quiet, letting him talk first.

"That's a long drive to make for someone who isn't serious about a girl," Grant says.

"Yes, it is, so it's a good thing I'm very serious about Ella."

"If you're here to have a big conversation with me, let's get it out of the way now, so we can both enjoy your time here."

Blunt and to the point. Okay, well, here goes nothing.

"Well, I had planned to ask your permission to court your daughter. I've spent the last month getting to know her and have just fallen in love with her. The distance is hard but knowing she's mine and we're working toward a future, would make it all worth it."

"And if I say no?"

My heart sinks. Is that what he's saying? I couldn't make Ella pick between her family or me. I know how close she is with her family but at the same time, I can't let her go either.

"As much as I respect you, it wouldn't stop me from still getting to know her. I'd respect your rules and hers, but I'm not going anywhere. There's something special between her and me. The once in a lifetime kind of special, and I'm not willing to walk away from that."

We walk in silence for a few minutes before he finally speaks.

"You aren't the type of man I had hoped my Ella would fall in love with. I always pictured her with someone from the church, staying here in town where we could have weekly family dinners and watch our grandkids grow up. I never thought I'd see her with a bar owner in Texas."

My heart races. I'm trying to think of what to say to convince him no one will ever treat Ella as well as I will when he speaks again.

"Her mother and I agreed a long time ago we would let our kids choose their path. I see the way Ella's face lights up when she talks to you. I don't think she realizes it, but she's slowly planning her life in Texas. I catch her saying little things here and there. I've come to find you a good man. You've respected our wishes, and I'll admit to calling Sage and getting every dirty detail about you, of which there were very few." He looks off ahead of us.

"I had a feeling this conversation was coming when you got here, and her mother and I talked about this last night. You have our blessing, but it's still Ella's choice."

I stop walking and gasp in some air. I can't believe what's going on. I thought I would have to fight for her, and I was prepared to do so. But knowing I have her father's permission is such a weight off my shoulders.

He pats my back and smiles. He knew exactly what he was doing, and I can't help but smile.

"Around here, asking to enter a courtship has as much fanfare as the engagement. The men go all out and make it this huge special moment, so I suggest you get to planning."

All I can do is nod.

"I also better tell you then since I saw Ella didn't, she had a run-in with a guy at church a few weeks back. He's new to the church and wouldn't leave her alone when she asked. She's fine. She got to me, and I sent him on his way, but I can tell he's interested in her. I know his type. He won't back down. The church leaders have already talked about him. No one knows much about him other than he met our pastor at some event about a year ago."

There's a sinking feeling in my gut, and it must have matched the look on my face because Grant is quick to reassure me.

"She never goes anywhere alone as it is but even more so when we go to church now. She goes with me or her brother, and many of the church elders are watching her and have an eye on him as well."

"Will you keep me updated on him even if I'm back home? I'd like to know if he doesn't leave her alone."

"Of course," he says as we turn back to the house. He shows me the guest house where I'll be staying and lets me get settled in before dinner. All I can think about is some asshole thinking he has a claim on my Ella.

Chapter 6

Ella

Jason has been here for three days now, and I love having him here. Yesterday, he took Maggie and me up to Nashville for the day, and we toured Andrew Jackson's home and the Belle Meade Plantation. We had lunch there and came home. We had a fun time, and Maggie tells me he's a good guy. She likes being our chaperone.

Mom had mentioned the covered bridge auto tour to Jason, and he suggested we go drive it tonight after dinner. Mom and Dad are both coming with us, and we're giving Jason a tour of the area. Jason insisted on driving, so Mom and Dad now cuddling in the back.

The conversation is going easily for the first two stops, and we make it to the third stop as the sun starts to set. This one you can't drive through anymore, but you park and walk through. It's been a while since I visited, so I'm excited to see it at sunset.

Mom and Dad walk behind us and as we get closer, I see the inside of the bridge is done up in hundreds of twinkle lights. Royce and Maggie are standing in front.

"What are they doing here?" I ask as we walk up.

"Let's go find out," Jason says with a smile on his face. Oh, he's up to something. I can feel it.

"Hey ladybug," Royce says and hugs me.

"What are you doing here?"

"Oh, we're playing fairy godmother," Maggie says.

Jason still has a huge smile on his face. He tilts his head toward the bridge. "Walk with me?"

I look back at my parents who are smiling, and they nod too. I nod to Jason and follow him into the bridge.

After a few steps in, he says, "I've really enjoyed my time getting to know you, and our phone calls are the best parts of my day."

I melt at that. "Mine too."

"Good because I'm hoping there's going to be a lot more. I knew when I was planning this trip, there was one big thing I wanted to have happen. I've already talked to your dad, so now I want to ask you."

He stops and takes a deep breath. When he faces me, I can tell he's nervous. He hands me a thin velvet box. When I open it, I see a necklace. The charm is of Texas and Tennessee with a heart over Texas and another heart over Tennessee and a swirly dotted line connecting them.

My eyes tear up. This one necklace describes how I feel to a tee.

"Ella, would you allow me the honor of officially courting you?"

That's when I lose it. "Yes," I whisper and don't even try to stop myself. I throw myself into his arms for a huge hug. He wraps his arms around me and holds me tight. He buries his head into my neck.

A moment later, I hear Dad clear his throat, so I pull away and wipe the tears from my eyes.

"Sorry, I wasn't thinking," I say.

Jason smiles and looks at Dad.

"I take it she said yes?" Dad jokes.

"Yes, sir. What are the rules for courting?"

"Well, they're what we make them as long as we all agree," Dad says.

"Can I negotiate hand holding?" Jason asks. I smile and nod.

"That would be fine," Dad says.

Jason's face lights up in a huge smile as he reaches out and takes my hand. I watch his hand wrap around mine, and he intertwines our fingers and rubs my hand with his thumb. When I look up at him, I see he's also looking at our hands.

When he looks at me, he says, "As much as I loved that hug, it's probably best we stick to side hugs."

"I agree," Dad says.

"I'd also like to keep the group texts. I want you to see I have her best interests at heart as we move forward," Jason says.

"I appreciate that. I think we can give you a bit more space on dates, walking behind you instead of with you and staying in eye distance that sort of thing."

"Sounds good to me," I say.

We walk the bridge, holding hands the whole time. Even on the car ride home, he holds my hand the whole time. We pull into the house, and I stop him before he heads off to his guest room.

"There's a church service tomorrow. A visiting pastor is in town, giving a sermon.

Will you go with me?" I ask, suddenly nervous.

"I'd like that. I want to see your church. It's such a big part of you. What should I wear?"

"Khakis and a nice shirt?"

He smiles. "I actually brought some in case I needed them. Good night, sweetheart."

"Good night, Jason."

Chapter 7

Jason

Ella's church is a night and day difference from the church back home in Rock Springs, Texas. The event space alone is huge. The guest speaker wasn't bad, and he knew how to tell a story for sure. Now we're at the reception afterward and thank God there's food. Good food! These church ladies sure do know how to cook.

I'm standing next to Ella, holding her hand, of course, as she introduces me to anyone and everyone who stops to talk to her. I'm looking around the room when a guy across the room catches my eye. While he's dressed the part, he looks very out of place, kind of how I guess I look. What catches my eye is how intently he's staring at Ella. So much so, it makes me uncomfortable. I wonder if this is the guy her dad was telling me about.

When the couple in front of us leaves, he beelines for us.

"Ella, who is that guy heading this way?" She looks around then I notice her eyes get big when she sees him.

"That's Seth," she whispers.

Seth.

I hate that name, and that means he's the guy her dad told me about.

"Ella baby, who is this?" he asks.

"She's not your baby." I snap at him. I was going to try to be nice, I was. No one gets to call her baby but her family and me.

His eyes snap to mine, and his eyes are cold. I feel Ella's grip on my hand tighten, and I use my thumb to rub her hand, trying to let her know everything is okay. When his eyes move back to her, I feel her step back and slightly behind me. I hate how uncomfortable his guy makes her but happy at the same time. She trusts me enough to know I'll protect her.

"Ella, I'm hurt. Didn't you feel that you were meant to be mine?"

"Funny. When you met her, she had already been mine for weeks."

"Then why is this the first time I'm seeing you?"

"Because I don't live here. My family owns a ranch in Texas."

He snickers. "Come on, Ella. You don't want to be a *rancher's wife*," he says it like it's a dirty word.

Deep breaths. I don't want to live up to the reputation of a bar owner by punching this guy in the face in the middle of the church's event hall.

I squeeze her hand, and it seems to be all the strength she needs.

"You don't know me, so you don't get to tell me what I want. It just so happens I can't wait to be a rancher's wife," she says.

My eyes snap to hers, and my heart races. I'd make that happen today if I could. I need to make sure she knows that when all this is done.

"You were meant for better things than that, Ella."

"As the lady said, you don't know her," I growl. "I think it's time for you to move on," I say.

He glares at me and eyes up Ella. "This isn't over," he says.

"Yes, it is," Grant says from behind us. I hadn't heard him come up. "Ella is spoken for, and our family wants nothing to do with you if this is how you pursue a woman."

Seth's back straightens and with one last look at Ella, he walks away.

I turn to Ella and wrap my arm around her shoulder and fight every instinct that says to pull her to me. "You okay, sweetheart?"

She nods. "Something about that guy just scares me every time he's near."

I glace over her head at Grant. "I don't have a good feeling about him either."

Grant nods "That makes two of us."

"Daddy, can we leave?"

"Yes, Maggie is ready to go as well. She can go with you."

"Why don't we get some ice cream?" I ask and watch Ella's face light up.

"That sounds perfect!"

Later that night, I call Colt and ask him about the private investigator he used when Sage was in Tennessee helping Abby who was having trouble with her parents' church after they died. He sends me the info, and I shoot off an email with everything I know about the guy, saying I'm not sure what I'm looking for, just any information he can get me. I get a response saying he'll start on it and call me tomorrow.

• • • ● • ● • • •

I'm sitting on the couch in Ella's parents' living room and just watching TV with my girl. I leave tomorrow and every time I think about it, I feel like I'm ripping my heart out. My heart will be staying here in Mountain Gap, Tennessee, but my body will be in Texas. That necklace I gave her the night I asked to court her couldn't be truer. Speaking of that necklace, she hasn't taken it off, and I smile every time I see it on her, a part of me on her. The only thing that could be better is my ring on her finger.

We've spent the last few days talking about anything and everything pertaining to a life together. The biggest thing we covered is what rules we would have in our marriage. She wants the option to wear jeans, which I'm okay with. I encourage her to go back to school and work with Megan, and she likes that idea.

We talk about kids, how many we want, how we will raise them, and if we want them homeschooled on the ranch or sent into town each day. We talk about the type of wedding we'd have, who we'd invite and where we'd have it. I suggest getting married here in Tennessee, but she wants to get married at the ranch church where we'll be starting our lives. I fall in love with her a bit more.

We haven't said the big 'L' word yet, but I'm there and I plan to tell her how I feel face to face before I leave tomorrow. In fact, I think a good walk tonight is in the cards.

I can't even tell you what's playing on the TV, but it's some movie my angel wants to watch, so I gladly sit here and soak in time with her and watch her watch TV. Her mom comes in and sits down, so I turn to Ella.

"Hey sweetheart, I'm going to talk to your dad for a minute. I'll be right back, okay?"

"Okay. Hurry back so you don't miss the good part," she says, not taking her eyes off the TV.

I smile. "Wouldn't dream of it."

I walk to her father's office and even though the door is open, I knock on the doorframe. When he looks up, he smiles.

"Come on in, Jason," he says.

I close the door behind me and take a seat in the chair across from him.

"What's on your mind?"

"To be honest, the dread I feel having to leave here tomorrow."

He chuckles. "I know that feeling well. I still get it when I have to spend any time away from my Maria."

"I'd like to see if your family can come down to Texas again sometime soon. If not the whole family, whoever can make the trip."

"Well, I don't know..." I don't let him finish.

"I'll cover all expenses if that's an issue. Flying would be faster."

He smiles and shakes his head. "Let me finish, son. I was going to say I don't know our schedule but if you give me a minute, I can pull it up. Maria and I keep our calendars synced."

I watch him pull out his phone and check his schedule.

"Well, we can come down for a four-day weekend in two weeks."

"Yes, tell me what I need to do to make it happen."

"Just make sure there's a church we can go to on Sunday morning."

"You can come to church with my family. Not everyone goes every week, but Mom and Dad do, and so do Sage and Colt."

"That sounds good. Have you talked to Ella about this?"

"No, I didn't want to get her hopes up if it didn't work out."

"What do you think about not telling her and surprising her?"

I smile. "I like the idea. She won't be mad, will she?"

"No, she'll be too excited to be mad."

I laugh. Then I get to thinking about what I want to plan while she's back on the ranch again.

"Something else on your mind?"

"Well, how long does courtship normally last?"

Grant leans back in his chair, studies me for a bit, and doesn't say anything at first.

"Normally a few months, why?"

I nod, taking it in. A few more months before I can ask her to be my wife, to be mine.

"Well, she's it for me. I know it, and I'll give her the time she needs, but I'll be asking for her hand real soon, so this is just a head's up on where I stand."

He's quiet again, watching me before saying, "Well, I like you being open and honest. You've given me a lot to think about."

The rest of the day is spent relaxing together, watching some more TV, and talking. After dinner, I suggest a walk to enjoy the sunset, and her mom and dad agree. They would like to go, so now we're walking and they're behind us, out of earshot. I know they have their eagle eyes on us.

"I hate that you're leaving tomorrow," Ella says, and the sadness I hear in her voice is enough to break me.

"If I didn't have to go back, I wouldn't. I'd never spend a day away from you."

She gives a sad smile. "I know, and I feel the same way."

I stop walking and turn her to face me. "Good because you're it for me, Ella." I tuck a finger under her chin and tilt her face up to mine. "I love you, Ella," I say barely above a whisper.

Her eyes water. "I love you too, Jason." She takes my hands, giving them a firm squeeze.

She nods her head. "We can do this."

"We can." We start walking again. "Your dad said courtships are a few months, but I'm warning you. Ours will be short. I don't think I can't wait that long to make you mine."

She smiles. "I can't wait to be yours."

"Good, because I love you." Now that I've said it, I can't seem to stop.

"I love you too." She laughs, and it's a sound I wish I could bottle up for the hard times ahead.

We spend the rest of our walk talking about family and how ranch life is. She's excited to learn how it all works and tells me how much she loved horseback riding when she was at the ranch last time.

I send up a silent prayer that many more nights like this are in our future.

Chapter 8

Jason

I lie in bed, not wanting to get up just yet. I want to stay in the warmth of the dream I just had of my angel. She was here on the ranch and in my arms. She was mine to hold, to touch, and to kiss. The best part? Her belly was round with my child.

The dream was so simple, but it was everything. Ella was sitting on my lap on the front porch, and I was rubbing her stomach, playing with our child who would kick my hand over and over. Ella laughed, and I couldn't keep the smile off my face. I looked up at Ella and a second before her lips met mine, I woke up.

Not only did I wake up, but I woke up with a hard-on and the worst case of blue balls. No matter how many times I take care of myself when I wake up, in the cold shower, before bed, it is never enough. I don't think it would ever be enough until it's her.

Even though I know it won't help, I take myself in my hand and stroke my hard cock up and down. I close my eyes and think of the dream Ella round with my child, her breasts fuller and at eye level. Then I change the dream.

I pull her top down to expose one of those milky tits and take it into my mouth and suck hard, causing her to gasp and arch her back, followed by a moan. I slip my hand under her skirt to find her soaking wet for me.

I squeeze my dick harder and stroke faster as I think of sliding my fingers into her soaking-wet pussy and thrusting in and out of her. I increase my stroking, and my stomach muscles tighten as I come all over my belly in hot spurts.

The relief lasts only minutes before my phone goes off, and I see a good morning text from her. My balls ache all over again.

Ella: Good morning! What's on the agenda today?

Well? Cleaning up cum on my stomach from jacking off to fingering you for one. But

I don't think she or her parents would appreciate that text.

Me: Helping Sage unload a new horse today before heading into the bar. Have payroll today. Loads of fun. What about you?

I get up and head in to take a quick and very cold shower, which doesn't help matters one bit when I see a have not just a text but a picture from her.

The photo is of her standing in front of her garden, and she's smiling at me a bit shy. Fuck, I'm rock hard again.

Ella: Gardening today and then I'm volunteering at the animal shelter.

I save the photo to my phone before I reply.

Me: Playing with puppies is the best volunteer work.

Ella: It really is.

She includes several laughing face emojis.

We text a bit more about some of the animals at the shelter as I get ready to head downstairs.

It's been a week since my visit with Ella. This time away from her is killing me even though I know in a week, she'll be here with me again. Even just for a few days, it still might as well be years away.

Just as we're finishing up breakfast, the private investigator calls with an update on Seth.

"Tell me you have something, Ozzy," I answer the phone.

"Well, I have something in the fact that I *don't* have anything." The man on the other end takes a drag from his cigarette.

"Please explain."

"The man known as Seth Covine with the information he registered at the church with, doesn't exist."

"Okay, now what?"

"Well, in my line of work, that means he's running from something. You and your girl both said you get a bad vibe from him. I'd say your gut is right, and you need to stay away."

"How do we find out who he really is?"

"That's as easy as it is hard. We just need his fingerprints. But since I'm willing to bet he won't give them up willingly, I have an idea."

"What is it?"

"I have someone pose as someone interested in the church at an event he's at. We keep eyes on him then swipe a glass he drinks from. This won't only give me his fingerprints but his DNA."

"Do it. Just don't let anyone know who you are, why you're there, or who hired you. I haven't told my girl's family yet."

"Sounds good. My sister will be the one going in. I figure a little flirting will be a good distraction, and she'll cause less attention than I would, at a church anyway. I'll be in touch."

When we hang up, a wave of unease washes over me. My gut was right about Seth, but we have no idea what he's running from. It could be something as simple as a stalker, but I have a feeling it's more along the lines of something more sinister.

To take my mind off it, I head over to my parents' house. Mom is at the beauty shop today, gossiping with the old ladies and Megan. I smile thinking about it. I know Ella will love Megan's shop, and I can't wait to show it to her when she's here.

When I get to my parents' house, I find Dad in his study, reading. He has always had an open-door policy and insists family never needs to knock, but I still do on the doorframe to get his attention.

Dad's office is huge, and he has floor-to-ceiling windows that overlook the barn, so he can see what's going on. The chair he likes to read in is next to these windows on the other side of the room, so I doubt he heard me come in.

"Jason! How are you, son?"

"Good, Dad, how are you?" I walk into the room.

"Well, honestly, it's a bit too quiet here with your mom gone into town." He chuckles.

"Well, I was hoping for your help with something."

"Anything."

That's one of the many amazing things about Mom and Dad. They don't care what us kids need help with, they're there and will support us. It's never come up, but I'm willing to bet it wouldn't matter if it were legal or not.

"Well, I need to go ring shopping."

I watch a huge smile cross his face. "Oh, it's about time. I knew that Ella was a special one. It is Ella, right?"

I laugh. "Yes, Dad, it's Ella. I think it'll be a little bit before I ask, but I want to be ready."

"Oh, I know that feeling. I had your mom's ring in my pocket for two months before I finally asked." He stands and heads across the room. "I know just the place to look. They have great vintage stuff too. Not that stuff you find in stores that are cookie cutter of what ten thousand women have."

I knew Dad would understand what I needed.

Chapter 9

Ella

It's been two weeks since I last saw Jason. I've asked him about when we can get together again, and he's beating around the bush, something about promotion from the TV show and tells me as soon as he knows, he'll tell me.

Today, my family is leaving to speak at a church, but I'm not sure where, and I didn't pay much attention. We go to these several times a year. I've been texting with Jason all morning. I guess one of Sage's horses gave birth last night, so he's been sending me a ton of photos of the momma and baby. Let me tell you, baby horses are just so cute.

His last text was a video of the baby walking around on shaky legs before falling, and I've been watching it repeatedly. We head to board the plane. I tell Jason we're heading to our seats, so he asks me to text him when I land.

We get into our seats, and I pull out my headphones and turn on a movie I've been waiting to watch on the plane and drown out the outside world.

• • • ● ● ● ● ● • •

I'm so zoned out watching the movie, I don't realize we're landing until I feel the wheels touch down. It's perfect timing; there are only five minutes left in my movie. Once finished, I send Jason a quick text letting him know we landed, but I don't get anything back right away.

I gather my bag and follow my family out. We head out of the main security area when I look up, and I can't believe my eyes. There standing with all the others waiting for people to get off their planes is Jason with his hands in his front pockets and the biggest smile on his face.

After a minute of shock passes over me, I drop my bag and run to him, kind of like in the movies but I just can't wait to be in his arms another minute. I know I need to stop and restrain myself and do a side hug but at this point, I don't care. It's been a miserable two weeks with my heart gone, and I just don't care anymore.

I launch myself into his arms and wrap my arms around his neck. He catches me and wraps his arms around my waist and rests his head on my shoulder.

"Why didn't you tell me?!"

I feel him laughing as he sets me down. "That greeting was well worth the hard time I had keeping it a secret, sweetheart."

I step back from him, blushing. I can't believe I did that. I look over and see Dad shaking his head and handing me back my bag.

"That was one heck of a side hug, Ella," he says with a smirk, and I'm sure my face gets even redder.

Jason reaches out and takes my bag in one hand and my hand in the other.

"Any other bags to get?" he asks.

"Nope, this is it," Dad says.

We head out with Mom, Maggie, and Royce following behind us.

"Dad let me borrow his truck so we can fit everyone, but it's still going to be a tight squeeze," Jason says.

We load our bags in the back and then all look at Dad for how he plans to do this. Someone will be bumping elbows, sitting next to Jason.

"Ella, get up. You can sit with Jason, but I'll be right next to you, so no funny business."

I smile just as big as Jason does. "Promise, Daddy," I say and kiss his cheek as I get in. Mom, Maggie, and Royce squeeze in the back row.

We spend the drive out to the ranch talking about his plans for the weekend. He has some horseback riding lined up, a trip to Megan's shop, a date night tomorrow, and what sounds so nice to me right now is some time with the new baby horse when we get in.

"So, Jason, what's going on at WJ's?" Dad asks.

"Well, we started work on an outdoor seating area. We need the space now as it stands and like Ella stated, it will allow for a more family friendly area. Plus, once the show premieres in a few months, we expect to see an increase then too. We plan to open for lunch to test the waters. Nick has been testing out some sandwiches. He's looking forward to you guys trying out if you're up for it."

"I'd like to see the place, and I'm always up for some good food," Dad says. "You'll have to let us know when the show is supposed to air. We want to watch it."

"As soon as I know, I'll let you know."

"Ella has been talking about this baby horse you've been sending her pictures of all morning," Maggie says.

"Well, it's called a foal since the horse is under a year old. I figure it will be our first stop. You'll have to wrestle time away from Megan and Hunter."

"Why's that?" Mom asks.

"Well, a few months ago, one of the cows had twins. Megan was the only one here, so she called Hunter for help. That night was the start of their relationship. They bonded over those twins and have been inseparable ever since. So, they take special notice of any babies in the barn now. It's kind of their thing."

"They're getting married soon, aren't they?" I ask.

"Yes, next month. You'll be my date to the wedding, right? You're all invited. Megan will have my hide if you aren't there."

Mom laughs "Yes, she has already talked to me. We have it on the calendar."

"So, since we'll be here, of course, I'll be your date," I say.

"Good, I can't wait. Maybe I can get you to dance with me?" he asks, and my stomach flutters. Being in Jason's arms is something I want more than anything every day.

"With a respectable distance apart, I don't see why a good waltz wouldn't be acceptable," Daddy says.

We get to the ranch, and Colt and Mac meet us at the truck.

"They're going to take your bags to your rooms, the same rooms as last time," Jason says.

He takes my hand, and the electric shocks shoot up my arm as he leads me into the barn. We walk past a few stalls to one slightly larger and when I look in, I see the momma horse and her foal. The foal is lying on the ground right next to his momma, who is eating some oats right now.

She watches us closely as we check out her baby.

"Sage has named this little one Kit Kat because of her light and dark brown colors."

"I like that name. I think it suits her."

After our time in the barn, Jason lets us head upstairs and get settled in before dinner. After dinner, we head back out to the barn and spend some more time with Kit Kat. Sage comes out and tells me about the birth and that she plans to train her as a show horse.

We call it a night after that since it's been a long day of travel, and I can't wait to see what he has in store tomorrow.

Chapter 10

Jason

Ella is spending the morning with her mom and Sage getting a garden set up. It's been a running joke with everyone that Sage is a damn fine rancher, but she doesn't have a green thumb. Mom has been over there helping them. While she has only grown flowers and some herbs, she's excited to help and grow some vegetables too.

They're planning to grow tomatoes, peppers, eggplant, potatoes, asparagus, broccoli, onions, and carrots. The guys and I veto the Brussel sprouts. Mom is mad, but then I point out none of us have seen her eat one. She huffs and walks off, making all of us smile.

They have us men out there digging and setting bricks for the small fence to hold the soil. Blaze has Riley planted on a blanket, watching everything. He has been spoiling her and not letting her lift a finger since she told him she's pregnant at their wedding a few months back. She has let him too, always just shaking her head and smiling. Right now, she's watching us finish the second row of bricks and rubbing her newly showing baby bump.

Blaze must notice it too because he stops working and stalks over to her, his knees hitting the ground just as he reaches her.

"Wife," Blaze says.

Riley smiles and looks up at him. "Husband."

He growls and slowly lays her down on the blanket and rests his forehead on her lower belly. "I really like this bump. I need to feed you more, so it grows faster."

Riley laughs. "I don't think that's how it works."

Blaze lifts his head and puts his mouth right next to her bump. He does this often, talking to the baby. "Tell Mommy that Daddy is right. The more I feed you, the faster you'll grow, so I can start feeling you move." He leans down and kisses her belly before sitting back up and getting Riley's water. "Drink up, baby."

I hadn't heard Ella come up beside me until she bumps her shoulder into mine. "They're really sweet."

"I can't wait to have that," I say without thinking.

"Me either," she says.

I look down at her and smile. "For the record, I plan to have that with you."

She laughs. "That's good to hear because I plan to keep you around for a while."

Before I can say anything, Sage says, "Good because we're going to keep you around, even if we have to chain you to the garden. You might be the only one who will keep it alive."

We all laugh.

"Want to go with me to check on Kit Kat before lunch?" Sage asks Ella.

"Yes!" Ella squeals, causing me to smile.

While Mom and Riley make lunch, we all clean up. I'm taking Ella and her family into town after lunch. We're going to visit Megan, walk the shops, and show them the bar. That part I'm nervous about. I want them to like it.

No, correction. I honestly want Ella to like it. As my wife, she'll be there weekly I'm sure, and I want her to enjoy it.

On the way into town after lunch, I explain to them how Megan came to take over the shop.

"The owner, Betsy, had no one to leave it to and When Megan started working there in high school cleaning and working the desk they got to talking and Megan said she'd love to own a shop but since we were saving to buy Sage's family land the money wasn't there," I tell Ella and her family.

"Of course, she never mentioned this to us because we would have made it happen. I think she knew that and that's why she never brought it up." I laugh.

"Well, Betsy wanted Megan to take it over, so she made some stipulations she had to get licenses then go back to school for a business degree. As she reached certain milestones with her school she signed over more and more of the business to her. Once she graduated she signed over the last of the shop. That was just a few months ago."

"Wow, I'm even more excited to see the shop now, knowing the story behind it!" Ella bounces in her seat, causing me and her dad to laugh.

I park around back near Megan's truck, and we head in. Of course, everyone stops to look at us; this is gossip central after all. Thankfully, I warned Ella and her family about that, so they're just smiling now.

"Hey!!" Megan calls out when she sees us. "Give me five to finish Grace's hair, and I'm all yours!"

"Take your time," I say.

Royce steps up beside me and nods to the back chair. "Who's that?"

"Oh, that's Anna Mae. She's only here temporarily. She just went through a divorce, found her husband cheating on her, and she's staying with her grandma here while the divorce was finalized. I heard it was last week, so now she's just trying to get back on her feet."

Royce nods, but he hasn't taken his eyes off her. It reminds me of how I look at my Ella. Interesting.

"Oh Grace, do I have your next appointment booked?" Megan says.

"Oh yes, I'm booked for the rest of the year, dear."

"I figured, but I always ask."

"I know. See you next week for my nails," she says and waves her fingers at Megan.

"Okay, big brother. I'm all yours." Megan turns to Ella. "I heard you do hair for weddings?"

"I do back home, but I'm not a professional or anything."

"Do you have any photos?"

"I do!" Ella's mom butts in and shows them off like a proud momma bear. It makes me smile at the love they have for their daughter.

"These are good, Ella. You have talent!" Megan gushes, and she isn't one to blow smoke up your ass, so you know she means it when she says it.

Ella blushes, which I find so darn cute. "Thanks."

"Let me show you around the shop." She takes Ella's hand, introduces her to everyone, and explains how certain things in the shop work and how they do certain things.

She shows her the stock room and her office, and I just watch Ella's eyes light up. She wants this, I can tell. That means it's my goal to make it happen. They go on to talk about schooling. I guess it takes eight months, and that sounds about right when I think back to Megan being in school.

Megan gets pulled away to talk to a client, and Ella bounces over to me and sits next to me.

"I love it here! I love the vibe and the people."

"How would you feel about working here?" I ask her.

Her eyes go wide. "Oh, I can't. I live in Tennessee. And I don't have any schooling."

I laugh. "Ella, we've been talking about getting married. You don't think that means you would be moving to Texas with me? Anna Mae won't be around much longer, so that chair will be waiting for you. There's the school Megan went to about twenty minutes from town. If this is what you want, I'll make it happen."

I watch her smile. "You'd be okay with me working? I thought you'd want me at WJ's with you."

I smile and shake my head. "I would love to have you by my side there but if this is what you want, this is what I want. The bar is just down the road. You can see it from the shop's front door. We could do lunch together then when you get done, you can join me or go home with Megan."

"You've thought about this, haven't you?"

If she only knew, it's all I think about. I wonder how badly that would scare her off. What I don't tell her is I'll probably be stopping in a few times a day just to kiss her and hold her. We've spent so much time apart, I'll have to remind myself she's real. That she's mine.

Megan comes back over, and we chat for a bit longer before her next client comes in. I notice Royce has spent most of his time talking to Anna Mae, and I know his mom and dad have noticed too.

I wonder which one is worse in the eyes of their church, a bar owner or a divorced woman. The church isn't bad; they just don't believe in divorce, so I'm not sure how that will affect Royce. I want to ask Grant later if I can get him alone.

When we leave Megan's shop, we walk down Main Street and check out the shops. There's a fun antique shop, a clothing boutique, a bakery, a resell or thrift shop, and one of those shops that take 'junk' and upcycles it into fun décor, or so Sage tells me.

As we near the bar, my nerves kick up. Her parents have been okay with the bar so far but still, I hesitate. What if they hate what they see and don't want their daughter anywhere near it? What if Ella hates it and changes her mind about me? There's no question in my mind. I won't give up Ella for anything, I'd give up the bar first.

Sorry, Waylon, I hope you don't hate me up there, bother. Well, if I'm being honest, I don't think Waylon is in heaven. He always said it would be too boring. He wanted to give the devil a run for his money.

That thought causes me to smile as we cross the road to WJ's. Once in the parking lot, I stop and take it in. It doesn't look like much from the outside. Just the same old honky-tonk bar you find in any old small town. On one side, we've taken over some of the parking lot to make the outside seating. The deck is already in, and the railing is going up now.

I lead everyone over that way first.

"This is the outdoor seating area. There's going to be a canopy over it. The sides will be clear and can be opened during the good weather and closed during bad weather. There will be heaters for when it's too cold and cooling misting fans for the Texas summer heat."

I watch Grant take it in.

"Will it be full service out here?"

"Well, yes, those windows next to the door will be opened with screens so the live music can be heard the nights that we have some. You'll be able to get food and drinks from the bar, but we'll encourage anyone who is just drinking to do it inside."

"How many people will you be able to sit out here?"

"About fifty. A few more if we squeeze tables together for larger parties."

"How many can you seat inside?"

"We seat about one twenty-five at the tables and another twenty at the bar. It doesn't fill up unless we have the live music on Friday and Saturday nights or a special show."

"That a lot for a small town," Grant says.

"Yes, but the next closest bar is in a twenty-mile radius of here and if you go west, it's thirty minutes. We get a lot of the ranchers and towns nearby too. We draw more of a crowd now that Nick has won the BBQ award too."

"Well, let's take a look inside," Grant says, and I know he's being critical. I'm the man who plans to take care of his daughter. I may have the ranch to fall back on and my family, but when you're going to hand your daughter off to someone, you want them to be able to take care of her without their fallback plan.

I get it. I plan to be this critical with our daughters too. That thought makes my breath catch, and the thought from my dream that keeps replaying nightly fills my head. Ella round with my child, little girls running around, looking just like her. It's almost more than I can take.

Inside, I show them around and explain the wood on the walls comes from barns around the area, and the same with the brands from the local ranches. Grant looks impressed when I tell him I built out the bar to what it is now with the shelves and displays.

He just shakes his head at the red, white, and blue beer can flag on the wall behind the bar, but I see a hint of a smile on his face.

"Jason!" Nick comes out of the kitchen and greets everyone.

"Everyone, this is Nick, the BBQ genius who put this place on the map and a friend of mine from high school," I say as I introduce him to everyone. I notice his eyes linger on Maggie much longer, and a slight blush covers her cheeks when they shake hands.

"Well, if you're up for it, I have a few of my new dishes made for you guys to test out and to get Jason's final approval on." I notice Nick never takes his eyes off Maggie as he talks.

"Bring them out," I say with a smile on my face.

We try out his new cheese fritter appetizer with a honey mustard BBQ sauce, and everyone loves it, so it makes the menu. He has a new pulled BBQ taco for us to try with some citrus coleslaw, which is delicious too.

"The food alone is going to drive people in from Dallas, I'm willing to bet," Grant says.

"That's the plan," Nick says.

I give Grant a quick look at the books and talk financials a bit before we head home in time for dinner. Thankfully, everyone eats since Riley cooked. The last thing you want to try to do is to explain to a pregnant lady you aren't hungry, and that's why you aren't eating her food.

Trust me on this, I have firsthand experience.

When we all turn in, I walk Ella up the stairs to say good night.

"Tomorrow, we have a date for dinner, so decide who you want to bring with you, okay?"

"What kind of date?" she asks.

I smile. "A country date. I'm going back to my roots."

She laughs. "Okay, see you in the morning."

I watch her head down the hall and before I can think twice I call out.

"Hey, Ella?"

She stops and turns around. "Yeah?"

"I really like having you here."

She smiles "I really like being here. It…"

"It what?"

"It feels like home."

My heart swells. That's all I want is for her to feel happy and at home here.

"I love you. Get some sleep, sweetheart."

"Love you too, good night."

Chapter 11

Ella

I had a hard time falling asleep last night, knowing Jason was just down the hall. I wanted to run down and just fall asleep in his arms. I thought about how I told him this feels like home. It really does. I'm happy here, and I feel safe and at peace.

I love my parents' home, but this is where I feel like I'm meant to be. In having these thoughts, I realize I know I want to marry Jason. I know he's my forever, and I don't see the point in waiting. I don't know his thoughts on this, but I plan to talk to him about it. For this reason, I'm going to ask Sage to come with us.

I like Sage, and she's very levelheaded. I want to know his thoughts without my family butting in.

I spend the morning with Sage and her mom in the garden. We get the soil in and a planting plan lined up for them for when I'm gone. I spend some time with Sage in the barn with Kit Kat, who's growing faster than I expected. I love watching them.

Jason joins us for lunch, and he's unloading some things from the back of his truck, and I grab the fence for support. He's in jeans and a button-down orange, red, and white flannel that he leaves open and unbuttoned. He has an orange t-shirt underneath, and he's sexy as sin. Watching him jump out of the back of the truck and walk up to me, I can't even talk.

I think he knows it too. He has this cocky smile on his face, but it makes him even sexier and reaffirms my thoughts on needing to move this relationship forward a bit faster.

I talk to Dad at lunch about Sage chaperoning the date tonight, and he agrees. I guess he has had a strict talk with Sage about what is acceptable and what isn't.

Jason, Maggie, and I go horseback riding after lunch, and then Jason says he has some business to do. I spend some time watching TV with Riley and learning her story of meeting Blaze and coming into the family.

Now, I'm getting ready for date night in Sage's room. Sage is letting me borrow a dress of hers that's done in a gorgeous Aztec print that brings in turquoise and maroon. I put on a pair of black leggings under it and my boots. Megan is here doing my hair and makeup for me. Though I don't understand why I need makeup if the goal is to make it look like I'm not wearing makeup. But it makes them both so happy to be helping me get ready, I can't say no.

Sage is excited to be chaperoning the date. I think she's excited to tease Jason about being the oldest and needing to be chaperoned by his younger sister. I love how he pretends it annoys him, but I can tell he could care less when he's with me. It's how I feel about being with him.

As we head downstairs, the butterflies are back in my belly where they are every time I get to see him. We saw each other for most of the day, but tonight is a date. It's different from just hanging out and watching TV. This is planned and supposed to be romantic. Not to mention, I want to talk to him about us, and it has to be tonight while Sage is here.

We get downstairs and I find Jason talking to Dad, and he stops when he sees me. His mouth is open slightly, and his eyes are wide as I descend the stairs. He just watches until I reach the bottom and then moves towards me.

"Ella sweetheart, you are breathtakingly beautiful," he says, his voice hoarse.

I smile up at him and take in his dark jeans and a red button-down shirt with the sleeves rolled up and of course, his cowboy hat and boots.

"Hey, that's my dress, you know." Sage fake pouts. Jason smiles and shakes his head.

"It looks way better on Ella."

"Ya know, if you weren't in love, I'd be offended by that." Sage laughs.

Jason shrugs his shoulder, and it makes me laugh. He takes my hand and leads me out the door.

"Be good, Ella, and, Sage, keep an eye on them," Dad calls.

I nod, but Sage says, "I'll keep both eyes on them."

Jason groans. "Sage, just because you're married doesn't mean you can start with the corny dad jokes."

"Hey, I'm the adult here. I can be corny all I want tonight, children. Let's get a move on. I'm hungry."

Jason walks into the barn and out to the pasture by the house where the ranch truck is.

Once everyone is seated inside, he drives to the back tree line. It's only a minute or so drive but saves us some walking.

"What's in there?" I ask, pointing to the cooler he gets out of the back of the truck.

He smiles. "You'll see. Come on, just a short walk."

He takes my hand, and we walk through the trees before coming into a nice clearing. What I see takes my breath away.

To the side under one of the trees is a table set up with a white tablecloth, three chairs covered in white covers, and hanging from the tree must be dozens of lanterns with several more on posts around the table and the tree.

The table is set and even has some wildflowers in the center. There's a stand next to the table with a bucket of ice and what looks like champagne, but if I know Jason, that's not what it is. He knows I don't drink.

"Jason, this is beautiful!" I say as I take it all in.

When I look at him, he has his head down and is rubbing the back of his neck with his hand. He looks up at me from beneath his lashes.

"You like it?" he asks, sounding unsure.

"Oh Jason, this is beautiful!"

He smiles and seems to regain his confidence. He takes my hand, leads me to the table, and pulls out my chair for me. He then pulls out Sage's chair in the seat across from me, and he sits to my side.

Once seated, he opens the bottle in the ice stand, and I find out it's sparkling cider. He pours all three of us a glass then pulls out some appetizers.

"Oh, these are Nick's new cheese fritters?" I ask.

Jason smiles. "Yes, I know you liked them." He offers me the plate.

"I loved them. Sage, you have to try these."

We make small talk about the ranch and Kit Kat until he pulls out our meals.

"Mom's famous fried chicken with mashed potatoes, gravy, biscuits, and coleslaw."

I dig in. Every Southern girl loves fried chicken, and his mom's recipe is amazing.

After a minute, I decide it's now or never, like the Bon Jovi song. I don't want to lose my nerve.

"So, I've been thinking," I start, and that gets Jason's attention.

"About what?"

"I meant what I said last night. This place feels like home. It's not just the house, it's the people and the town. I love it here."

I watch his eye soften and a soft smile forms across his face. So I reach out and take his hand and take a deep breath.

"Being here this weekend just affirms for me that you're it for me. I can see myself here, a future, and a family."

I pause to gauge his reaction.

"What are you saying?" he whispers, never taking his eyes off me.

Taking another deep breath, I say, "I'm saying that I want what we've been talking about. The wedding, the family, the life. I want it all with you, and I want it sooner rather than later."

I sneak a glance at Sage out of the corner of my eye. She's still eating but has a smile on her face. She's trying to pretend she isn't listening but failing miserably.

Jason stares into my eyes, and a range of emotions crosses his. Then he nods. "Okay," he says and looks back at his plate.

OKAY?

I don't know what I was expecting but 'Okay' isn't on that list.

"Okay?" I ask, still a little stunned.

"Yes, okay is all I can give you right now. I want nothing more than to pull you into my lap right now and kiss you until your lips bruise and then haul you off to Vegas, so by morning, you have my last name. So please don't test control; it's on a thin wire right now, angel."

I look down at my plate, and I can't stop the smile that crosses my face if I tried. Thank goodness he has some control left. I know I wouldn't stop him if he did all those things to me. I think I'd give back just as much. It's all I've been thinking about since he came to visit me.

Chapter 12

Jason

It's bright and early Sunday morning, and I'm standing in church with my Ella next to me. Her family is next to her, and my parents, Sage, and Colt are on the other side of me. I've gotten a few stares but a lot of smiles. People have been coming over to introduce themselves before the service.

As Pastor Greg gives his sermon, my mind wanders back to last night. It took everything in me not to drop down to one knee and ask her to marry me right then and there, but I must do right by her.

That means having her parents' permission and doing it up right. A huge show of affection is what she'll get. I plan to make it over the top and a day she'll never forget. She's only ever getting married once, so I'll pull out all the stops.

I've already been texting with my family about my idea, and they all love it and want to help. I let the ladies of the family take charge and do what they do best. Sage is the most excited to help. We all helped in Colt's proposal to her, so this time she gets to be involved.

Ella insists on going to the potluck the church has after service every week. She wants to get to know the people in town. She and her mom spent yesterday making a 7-Up lemon bundt cake. I had to pull the puppy dog eyes to get her to make a second one for us at the ranch. It was so good, it was gone before bed that night.

Ella hid the cake for church and threatened a slow painful death to anyone who touched it. She'll fit in great around the ranch. The thought has me smiling like a fool. Ella catches me and elbows me, but I see a slight smile on her face too.

After service is over, we barely make it in the room for the potluck before the church ladies all descend on Ella and her family, wanting to know everything. I see Royce looking around the room and step over to him.

"Looking for Anna Mae?"

He sighs. "Yeah, there's just a connection there. I can't explain it, and I know my parents won't approve since she's divorced."

"Of no fault of her own. And you don't have to explain that connection to me. I feel it with Ella. If it's even half of what I feel with Ella, it won't go away. There's no point in fighting it."

He sighs "I was afraid of that."

"Just talk to your parents. I'm a bar owner, and your parents didn't turn their backs on me. Talk to them soon. The shop is closed today and tomorrow, so you might be able to spend some time with her before you leave."

I go back to rescue Ella from the church ladies, and we head over to get our food and sit down. Her parents, Royce, and Maggie aren't far behind. Soon as Royce sits down. he doesn't waste any time talking to his dad.

"Hey, Dad?"

"Yeah?"

"Do you remember Anna Mae from the shop the other day?

"Yeah, you two were getting along pretty good."

"I like her, Dad, and I want to get to know her and spend some time with her while I'm here. If she'll let me."

Grant sits back in his chair and crosses his arms. I've learned that this is his signature move when he's thinking about what to say.

"Isn't she divorced, son?"

Mom, who had just sat down, steps up.

"She is, Grant. She and her ex-husband lived in Dallas, and she went to visit him at work only to walk in on him having sex with his secretary. Not too long after, the secretary announced she was pregnant. Anna Mae was served divorce papers. She packed up and moved here to live with her grandma while she got back on her feet. Now she says she's trying to figure out her next move. She likes the town, but she said she doesn't have plans to stay."

Mom winks, and Royce blushes. I can't help but smile at that.

"Well, you have the same rule. Courtship is to be followed, group texts, and monitored phone calls. Also, I'd like to meet her officially before we leave. And maybe don't mention to the people at church she's divorced, not until it's a bit more serious."

I watch Royce's face light up, and he sits up a bit straighter like a huge weight has been lifted off his shoulders.

"Well, I can get Megan to invite her to dinner before you all leave," Mom chimes in.

"No need. She's at the ranch now. She and Megan are doing some online tutorial class thing. I invited her for dinner already. So, Royce here is your shot. She'll be there all day." Sage chimes in.

I don't think I've seen my family finish up at the church potluck so fast. If it had been me, they would have dragged it on for hours and been the last ones to leave. For Royce, we're out the door not thirty minutes later.

When we get home, Royce beelines for Anna Mae, and they get to talking.

I turn to Ella. "What do you want to do today, sweetheart?"

"I want to just be lazy. Maybe sit on the front porch a bit?"

Her mom and dad join us. Later, Royce and Anna Mae end up at the other end of the porch, talking. I have hopes of many more nights like this ahead.

Chapter 13

Ella

It's been two weeks since I saw Jason last, and we've been doing night video calls, which makes things a bit easier, but you just can't beat being there in person with each other.

We have plans to go back down as a family in two weeks for Megan and Hunter's wedding. Until then, I'm slowly going mad. I've run out of weeds to pull in the garden, and now I'm working on Mom's flower beds when I feel a shadow fall over me.

I look up to see Royce. He kneels and helps me before he speaks. "When are you heading back to Rock Springs?"

"In two weeks for Megan and Hunter's wedding. Why?"

He smiles.

"You've been talking to Anna Mae?"

"Every day," he says with a smile on his face.

"Do you see it going anywhere?"

"I don't know right now. I like spending time with her and talking to her. We have a lot in common, but I get the feeling maybe she's not looking for a relationship after her ex. I know she has trust issues, and I can't blame her."

"Maybe you should talk to Hunter. Megan wasn't ready for a boyfriend when they met, so he became her friend, and it worked out well for him. Be patient with her and show her you can go the distance."

"Yeah, maybe. So, where do you and Jason stand?"

"He's the one. We've talked about everything from marriage to kids. When we were there last, I told him I didn't want to wait anymore. I was sure, and I didn't care what the length of a normal courtship was."

"What did he say?"

"He changed the subject, saying if I kept talking like that, he wouldn't be able to not kiss me."

Royce laughs. "He's a good guy, I like him."

My phone rings, and I notice it's the church.

"Why is the church calling me?"

Royce takes my phone and answers it.

"Hello?"

I can't hear the conversation on the other end, but Royce looks pissed.

"I don't know who gave you this number, but you aren't allowed to call her until you have her father's approval, and I know you don't."

Who the heck could be on the other line? Who has my phone number?

"Well, I suggest you talk to her dad. This is your one warning not to call again. The last guy who did was slapped with harassment charges."

What is Royce talking about? I've never had anyone call me that I didn't know besides telemarketers. With them, I just hang up, no big deal.

When Royce hangs up the phone, he takes a deep breath and takes my hand.

"We need to go talk to Dad."

"Royce, what's going on? Who was that?"

"Seth."

I feel the blood drain from my face, and I can feel my body sway a bit as we walk into Dad's office.

"Hey, Dad?" Royce says.

"Hey, what's going on?" Dad asks with a smile on his face until he sees me.

"Seth called Ella's phone. It came from the church phone number. I was there and picked it up."

"How did he get her number?"

"He wouldn't say, but he was at the church when he made the call. I think he knew she would pick up a church call versus a strange number."

"And if he was at the church, he could have been snooping or gotten it from any number of people."

"Dad, everyone there would have given him your phone number. My guess is he was snooping and got access to it."

Dad is quiet for a few minutes, lost in thought.

"Ella Bear, don't pick up any calls from any strange numbers or the church. Only family and Jason until we figure this out, okay?"

I nod.

"Why don't you call Jason and let him know what happened? I'm sure he won't be happy to be kept in the dark on this."

I know this gets me out of the room, so Dad and Royce can talk, but I'm okay with that. I need to talk to Jason. I know he'll calm me.

The phone doesn't ring but three times before he picks up.

"Hello, Ella?"

"Hey, Jason."

"Hey, sweetheart, what's wrong? I can hear it in your voice."

I relay what just happened with Seth, and Jason is quiet.

"Say something," I whisper.

"Sweetheart, I'm so pissed off right now. Not at you, and I don't want you to think I am. Give me a moment to get my anger in check."

I hear him take a few deep breathes then a loud bang like something hitting the wall, and it makes me jump. It's quiet for a moment, then I hear ice in a glass.

"Okay. I'm sorry, Ella. I hate not being there."

"You okay?"

"Yeah, the wall not so much, but it can be fixed."

"Jason!"

He chuckles "I'm fine, sweetheart. I promise. Maybe you should think about changing your phone number. I don't like him having it."

I hadn't thought of switching my number, but I agree with Jason. I don't like him having my number either.

"I'll talk to Mom and Dad. I'm on their plan, so I don't know what it will take to do it."

"Well, make sure to tell him I'll cover any cost needed. I just need you to be safe."

"I promise to tell them, but I'm sure Dad will talk to you too."

I hear Jason sigh. "What are you doing today?"

"Well, I was working in Mom's flower beds, but I'm going to clean up and call a few friends to come over and bake with me. We're making cookies for a few groups my parents run at church."

"Well, I like cookies. Consider sending a care package. Mom isn't baking as much as she normally does and when she does? Riley ends up eating it all before I get home."

"It's the pregnancy. The baby likes it, and she can't stop eating it. I've seen it before. One girl ate a whole pie herself at church once, then pleaded with the lady who made it to make her more. By the time the lady brought them to her house the next day? She couldn't eat a bite. Her husband had to finish them off."

We talk for a few more minutes before getting off the phone.

I decide to call Vicky first and ask her to come over to help with the cookies. We haven't talked in a while, and I'm excited to fill her in with what's going on with Jason.

"Hello?" She sounds uncertain, but I know she has caller ID, the same as me.

"Vicky, it's Ella."

"I know. I'm just surprised you're calling, that's all."

"I don't understand. I'm just calling to see if you're coming over today to help with the cookies."

"Well, no."

"What? Why not?"

"Well, my parents won't let me hang out with you anymore."

"What? What did I do?"

"They heard you're being courted by a bar owner. They said it's not appropriate, and that he must be corrupting you. I'm not to be around all that."

"That's absurd. Even Jesus turned water into wine, you know."

She sighs. "Try telling that to my parents. I don't care who you're courting. If your parents approve, there has to be more to the story, but people are talking at church."

"Oh, I know how the rumor mill is."

"I'm sorry. I have to go."

"Thank you for at least telling me the truth."

"Of course, Ella. Best of luck."

I call Emma, Leah, and Livy and get the same response. Their parents have said they're to stay away from me.

I head inside to talk to my parents and find them in Dad's study.

"Hey Ella Bear, I talked to Jason. He mentioned getting you a new phone number, and we agree. You okay with that?" Dad asks.

"Fine, not like I have anyone to talk to anymore anyway," I mumble as I plop down on the couch.

Mom and Dad look at each other before coming to sit with me.

"What do you mean?" Dad asks.

"You aware of the gossip around the church?" I ask.

"No, can't say I've heard anything recently?" he says.

"Well, it's gotten around that I'm being courted by a bar owner and how he must be corrupting me. My friends' parents have all told them they aren't allowed to hang out with me anymore! Apparently, they're whispering about how you could let it happen."

Dad looks at Mom, as she sighs.

"I had heard a bit. Livy's mom asked if it was true. I said yes and didn't think much of it, but she hasn't talked to me since."

Dad shakes his head. "I was afraid of this. The church can't open their eyes and see past one aspect of someone, even when they've been told not to judge many times."

"Don't worry, Ella. If they aren't happy for you, you don't need them. Now let's make those cookies," Mom says.

I put on a fake smile and follow her to the kitchen.

Chapter 14

Jason

It's been a month since I last held my Ella in my arms, even if it was just a quick goodbye hug. Everyday talk and video calls just haven't been enough.

Ella's words from our date in the field still bounce in my head. We both know this is it, so why wait? I wanted to get down on one knee that night and ask her to be my wife. I wanted to sweep her off to the courthouse and marry her, so she never left. But I also want to do this right because she deserves that.

Today, I'm back at the airport, waiting for Ella and her family to get here for Megan's wedding this weekend. I get a whole week with her, and I can't be happier.

What Ella doesn't know is I've had many long talks with her dad over the last couple of weeks. I want a good relationship with him, and that takes time and bonding. I know it won't happen just because I'm going to marry his little girl.

I watch people file out of the airport security area and every time I see blond hair, my heart races. After the fifth time, I don't think I can take it anymore. God has mercy on me when I see her talking to Maggie with the biggest smile on her face.

When her eyes lock with mine, it's like no time has passed. Like there hasn't been a month since I saw her last. Everything and everyone in the airport fades away as she rushes to my arms just like last time.

There's no side hug. This is her body plastered to mine, her arms wrapped around me in the largest hug, and her face rests on my chest. I bury my face in her neck and take a deep breath.

"I missed you so damn much, sweetheart," I mumble into her neck.

"I missed you too, Jason. I don't want to leave."

"You just got here. We have a week. Let's not think about you leaving."

"Deal."

She pulls away and instantly, I hate the space between us. Her parents are there, and her dad is giving me the look. The one that says, 'you know what you did, don't do it again.' I haven't gotten that look from my own parents in over ten years.

I get them loaded up in the truck, and we head towards town.

"So, what's on the agenda?" Ella asks just as my phone rings.

"Can you answer that for me, sweetheart?" I ask her when I see it's Megan. "Put it on speakerphone."

"Hey Megan," I answer.

"Hey yourself. Please tell me Ella is there with you."

"I'm right here, Megan."

"Good. I need a huge favor. One of my bridesmaids backed out. I have her dress, but please tell me you'll do it. I promise to pair you up with Jason and everything. Just please, please, please say you'll do it!"

"Is that okay, Jason?" Ella whispers to me.

"Of course, sweetheart. I'd love nothing more than to be stuck next to you all day."

She laughs. "Well, I have to see the dress. Make sure it's modest enough," she says back to Megan.

"It's knee-length and modest. High neckline, but it's sleeveless. The girls all agree to wear whatever cover-up you need. Soon as you get here, I need to steal you away for a fitting and see what you need. One of the ladies from the beauty shop offered to tailor anything we need."

I just shake my head. This is so Megan.

"Okay, we're about an hour out," I tell her.

They say their goodbyes, and everyone laughs a bit once Ella hangs up.

"Sounds like it's going to be a busy few days," Ella's mom says. "Make sure you tell her I can sew and help with anything she needs as well. Okay, Ella?"

"Of course, Mom."

I take a deep breath and take Ella's hand. We talk about the wedding prep that has been going on at the ranch for the rest of the drive.

· · · · · · · · · ·

Ella

Megan is waiting on the front porch, and I barely get my feet on the ground before she's pulling me upstairs to Sage's room, which has become wedding headquarters.

"You're the most amazing friend, soon to be sister, and bridesmaid ever, ever, ever." Megan is talking a mile a minute, which shows me how nervous she is. It makes me smile. I hope to be in her shoes soon.

"Okay, show me the dress. Let's start there. OH! Mom wants you to know she can sew too if you need anything."

"Oh perfect! Let's see how this looks." She tosses a coral dress at me and pushes me towards Sage's massive bathroom.

As I get dressed, I take in Sage's bathroom with its hardwood floors and light-gray walls that play off the large rustic wood ceiling beams. It's done in a beautiful farmhouse style. The sinks are built into old dressers painted white. Even I'm jealous of her shower with the river rocks and rainfall showerheads.

When I'm dressed, I look at myself in the floor-to-ceiling mirror. The dress is a deep coral color and is knee-length. Plenty long. The neckline comes up to my collarbone, but it's sleeveless. It's very flowy and honestly, something I would wear out to a nice dinner.

"Open up before she kicks the door down." Sage laughs.

I open the door, and Mom is there taking measurements.

"I stopped in to see how you look. We'll need to do something about the sleeves, but the length is good. I just need to take it in a bit at the waist, but these wrap-around straps will help with the fit," Mom says as she pins the dress.

"The plan is to wear brown cowgirl boots. What about a lace sweater that is kind of see through?" Megan holds up her phone, showing a picture of the beautiful ivory lace sweater that you can see between the lace pattern.

"Oh, I like that. It's perfect," I say.

"Yay! Wendy has them in everyone's size, so I'm going to text Mom to pick them up. I think they'll look great with the dresses and the wildflowers."

"Megan?" I ask.

"Yeah?"

"Everything is going to be perfect. You have so much help, and now that Maggie, Mom, and I are here, you have even more."

She sighs and flops down on the couch at the other end of Sage's room.

"I know. I think it's more the excitement than anything. I can't wait to marry Hunter. I hid my feelings from even myself and now that they're out, all I want to do is shout it out to the world."

"Which you get to do the day after tomorrow," Sage says with a huge smile on her face.

"Okay, Ella, go change so I can get started on this dress," Mom says.

"Let me show you where the sewing stuff is. I don't use it much, so I put it all in one of the guest rooms," Sage tells Mom.

"Okay. With that, I'm off. Hunter and I have a date today. It's the last chance we have before the wedding, and Hunter is demanding some alone time with me," Megan says as she heads downstairs.

I smile and just take it all in. It's busy here, but the house is so big, you don't feel cramped, but you don't feel alone either. It's lived in, and I love that feeling. It gives me butterflies. I can't wait to live here too.

With any luck, it will be sooner rather than later.

Chapter 15

Jason

I wish I could say watching my little sister get married brought on this huge smile on my face. But I can't. In truth, I don't remember a thing about Megan's wedding ceremony other than she took a page out of Sage's book and had the couples stand together, spread out along the front of the church instead of guys on one side and girls on the other.

This means I get to stand by Ella for the whole ceremony. Her hand on my arm, her body leaning against mine, and I soak in every minute. I watch her as she watches the wedding. Every time she looks up and catches me looking at her, she blushes, and it's so damn sexy.

Megan has the wedding at the ranch church on the east side of the property. This church has been here for generations and has been brought back to life as Sage and now Megan both have gotten married here

After Megan and Hunter's kiss, I walk back down the aisle with my girl, and we head out for photos. Her parents are never far away from us the whole time. When photos wrap up, I get a bit nervous.

They're having their reception at the event barn on Mom and Dad's side of the ranch. This is where we not only have the yearly sale but have also seen many events for family and friends. Riley and Sage both had their receptions here, so it was a natural choice for Megan too. This is also the barn where I saw Ella for the first time several months ago.

The barn is the largest on the ranch and set up for events not for animals any longer. It was the original barn on the ranch but when it needed some massive repairs Dad built the new ones but never had the heart to tear this one down because of all the history it holds. It was Mom's idea to turn it into an event space when I was about 8 and it's been that way ever since.

Ella and I walk into the reception hand in hand, and I still can't find it in me to wipe the smile off my face. She's the most beautiful girl in the room in my completely biased opinion.

"You want something to drink, sweetheart?"

She smiles up at me. "Yeah, just a sweet tea. I'm going to find my parents."

"Okay, I'll join you in a few minutes."

I head to the bar and order two sweet teas for us and watch Blaze and Riley walk up to us. Blaze pulls Riley in front of him and rests his hands on her baby bump and kisses her temple.

"So, where's Ella?" Riley asks.

I nod off to the other side of the barn. "She went to find her parents."

"So, is everything set?" she asks.

"Yeah, I'm nervous, but Megan is so excited. You're going to use your baby bump and play defense, right?"

Blaze growls, but Riley laughs. "You better believe it."

"Good luck," Blaze says, and he and Riley head to their table.

I grab our drinks and make my way to the table Ella and her family are at. I set her drink down and smile.

"I'm having an odd sense of déjà vu," I say as I sit next to Ella.

"Me too." She smiles, and I can tell she's lost in thought just like I am, remembering that night we met.

We fall into an easy conversation over our meal and some of the traditions and finally, it's time for the bouquet toss.

"You better get up there," I say to Ella.

"Oh, this isn't my thing." She shakes her head.

"Come on, it's fun. You can't say no to the bride at her wedding." Megan comes up behind me, taking Ella's arm. She looks back at her parents who are smiling.

"She's right, you know. Go on, Ella Bear, have some fun." Her mom encourages, and I watch Megan pull her to the crowd.

Ella's family and I stand on the side to watch the whole thing play out. Megan pulls Ella to the front and center. Then I watch Megan head off to a spot not far in front. According to Sage, they've practiced this for days now.

Surrounding Ella is Sage, Riley, Mom, her mom, and her sister. Megan counts to three and on two, the girls push everyone backward, leaving a huge space for Ella to catch the bouquet when Megan tosses it. It all happens perfectly, Ella doesn't realize it was a setup until I'm in front of her and down on one knee.

When her eyes lock with mine, she lets out a small gasp, and her hand covers her mouth.

"Ella, I knew the day I met you in this very building, that you were the girl I had waited my whole life for. You were the one I was meant to spend the rest of my life with. What is life without a few curveballs, like us waiting for our wedding day for our first kiss?" I pause and smile when some of the crowd chuckles.

"I want to spend the rest of my life with you, I want to watch you go to school and tend the garden here on the ranch. I want to have kids and grandkids with you. I want to cook dinner with you and talk about our day. I want it all but only with you. Ella sweetheart, will you marry me?"

I take a deep breath and watch as my words sink in. Her eyes mist over, and I'm not prepared for her to throw herself in my arms and yell, "Yes!"

I catch her and hug her tight. When she pulls back, I put the diamond ring on her hand. When I saw the ring, I just knew it was her. It's an oval-cut diamond flanked with several other smaller diamonds on each side. I stand and hug her again and push my luck just a bit by kissing her temple.

"Hey Mr. DJ! Play that song for me!" Megan yells, and a slow song fills the barn.

"May I have the honor of this dance?" I ask Ella and hold my hand out to her. The look of pure happiness on her face is one I'll never forget and one I'll strive for daily.

I lead Ella out to the dance floor and tap into the old school dance videos I watched over and over on YouTube the last few days. I take her hand in mine and place her other hand on my shoulder and place my hand on her waist, keeping our frame within a respectable distance apart.

Then I slowly move us in the 1, 2, 3 waltz style dance. Ella takes right to it and after a few steps, she stops looking at her feet and looks up at me, her huge smile still in place.

"This is perfect. Megan was in on this, wasn't she?"

"Of course she was. She insisted when she heard I was planning to ask you to marry me."

"I want to get married here at the ranch church and the reception here. This is where we met. I think this is where we should start the next chapter in our lives too."

"I think it's perfect. You should talk to the girls. They all got married on the ranch, so I know they have tons of decorations and ideas already. When do you want to get married?"

"Tomorrow."

"If you girls can pull it off, I'll gladly marry you tomorrow." I laugh.

"I would say maybe a month? There isn't anyone other than my family I want at the wedding. Mom can do alterations on the dress. I don't want anything fancy. Something casual here is what I've been picturing."

"Whatever you want, you let us know, and we'll make it happen." The song ends and not wanting to push my luck, I lead her off the dance floor to the table her family is sitting at.

Immediately Riley, Sage, and Megan swarm the table to see the ring and talk about wedding plans. I see Blaze, Hunter, and Colt at the bar and make my way over to them. I pass Royce, who is sitting at a table with Anna Mae and her grandmother, and he stops me.

"Look like we're going to be family now. Maybe I should have given you this speech sooner, but I don't care if it's tomorrow or fifty years from now, you hurt my sister, I'll hurt you twice as bad."

"I'll bury anyone who hurts a hair on her head. She's the most important person in the world to me, and I won't let anyone hurt or upset her."

Royce nods. "That's what I want to hear." He nods toward the table where Ella is still surrounded by my sisters. "Wedding planning."

I laugh. "Yeah, I don't think Ella is going to want to wait too long. My sisters have plenty of experience with weddings at this point."

We chat for a few more minutes before I finish making my way over to the guys, and they congratulate me.

"So, you going to carry on the tradition to get married here on the ranch?" Blaze asks.

"I think so. Ella seems to want to get married at the ranch church and of course, have the reception here since this is where we first met."

"How soon?" Hunter asks.

"She joked about tomorrow but honestly, I'd say within a month easily."

After a few more minutes talking with the guys, I get Ella another sweet tea and head on over to brave the wedding talk with her dad.

Chapter 16

Ella

The next morning after Hunter and Megan's wedding, I wake to find both Riley and Sage sitting on my bed with a stack of bridal magazines spread out between the two of them.

"Hey sleepyhead, we were going to give you ten more minutes before waking you. We have a wedding to plan and limited time with you here! We stole Megan's wedding magazines for ideas," Sage says, holding up the one she was just reading.

I run my hands through my hair, sit up with my back against the headboard, and just watch them. They seem like they're talking to me but don't need an answer.

"So, tell us what you're thinking, so we can start planning!" Riley almost bounces off the bed.

"Well, I kind of want to do like Sage and Megan at the ranch church, and the reception has to be at the event barn since that's where Jason and I met."

I see Sage making notes on a notebook I missed earlier.

"Okay, colors? Themes?"

"Well, I want to keep with the rustic ranch theme you guys all had, but I want it to be relaxed. I saw these dresses I liked for bridesmaid dresses, but they aren't normal bridesmaid dresses. Let me get my phone."

I find my phone on the nightstand and pull up a dress I saved a few weeks ago. It's a maxi dress in a light blush pink with a fitted top covered in white lace down to the waist. The blush pink peeks out from the lace. It has the smallest cap sleeves, and I just love it.

"Oh my gosh, that's beautiful, Ella!" Sage says and passes the phone to Riley who agrees.

"Okay, so who are you looking to be in your wedding party. We'll need to get sizes today so we can order them," Riley says as Mom walks in the door.

"Oh, did you show them that dress you saved? The pink one?" Mom says.

"Yes, it's perfect!" Sage smiles as Mom sits down. "We were just asking her about the bridal party."

"Well, I'd like Maggie to be my maid of honor. Then, of course, both of you and Megan. That's it."

"No friends from back home?" Riley asks.

"None that still talk to me."

"What do you mean?" Sage asks, setting her pen and notebook down.

"Well, when it got out I was being courted by a bar owner, everyone has distanced themselves from me."

Sage frowns. "Well, we have a saying, 'Hard times show us who our true friends are. Love them and, ah, forget the rest.' That's the cleaner version." She laughs.

"What else?" Riley asks.

"I want to do this close to sunset. I want lots of twinkle lights everywhere. And one more thing, but it's a bit over the top."

"Ohhh, that means it's good! What is it?" Sage asks.

"I was thinking of riding up to the church on horseback in my wedding dress. The pictures with the sunset in the background would be amazing."

"I love it!" Riley says and claps her hands together.

"Well, this is going to be easy enough. Thoughts on food?" Sage smiles.

"There should be some?" I reply.

Everyone laughs. "Well, I want to make the cake," Mom says. "It's a side hobby of mine."

"And she's really good too!" I say and hug her.

"What about some ranch favorite recipes for dinner, keeping with the ranch and country theme?" Sage suggests.

"I love it."

"All right, next stop is the dress. We have an appointment in Dallas this afternoon, so get a move on." Everyone jumps up.

I can't believe she got me an appointment so soon! I get dressed in a green flannel shirt dress, which is quickly becoming my favorite things to wear around the ranch. I wear black leggings underneath and a thin brown belt with it. I pair it with my cowgirl boots and keep my hair and makeup natural. I head downstairs.

Jason is already downstairs when I make my way down. He sees me and meets me at the bottom of the stairs.

"Good morning, fiancée." He takes my hand and walks me into the kitchen.

"Good morning, fiancé," I reply and make myself a plate, but Jason pulls me to the table.

"Sit."

He fixes a plate with all my favorites and comes to sit beside me.

"I hear they're taking you wedding dress shopping today."

"They are, but I've no idea how they got an appointment so fast."

"Well, I've been planning this for a few weeks, so I'm guessing they made the appointment then, with the hopes you would say yes."

"Of course we knew she would say yes." Riley sits beside me. "Megan made us promise to video call her in. She wants to be there even though she can't be here."

"All right, girls, we need to head out just in case there's traffic!" Sage calls from the front door.

"I'll see you tonight. My guess is Sage will make this an all-day thing," Jason says as he stands and pulls me into a hug. "Text me or call. I'll have my phone on all day. I'm helping Colt over in the barn for a bit."

"Okay. I know nothing of the plans, but I guess I'll see you tonight."

On the way into Dallas, it's all wedding talk as Sage drives. Lots of details are ironed out. Everything but a date; that depends on the dress.

"You'll love this dress place. It's the same one all us girls have gone to. They have a huge selection, everything from vintage or modern," Riley says.

"Also I ordered those dresses for the bridesmaids. It's easy since we knew everyone's sizes," Sage says.

Maggie looks at me "You have your bridesmaids picked out already?" I see a bit of hurt in her face. We haven't talked about this yet.

"I only mentioned who I was going to ask. Maggie, you know you're going to be my maid of honor, right? You don't have a choice." Her whole face lights up, and she reaches over to hug me the best she can with our seatbelts holding us back.

"Of course I will. Who else did you ask?"

"Well, Riley, Sage, and Megan. There's no one else to ask."

"Yeah well, their loss."

I've talked a bit to my sister about why my friends back home aren't talking to me right now. She has made it her mission to hang out with me more and spend time together. We've always been close, but I think it has brought us even closer.

"Well, who is Jason having stand up with him? It has to be even," Sage says.

"I don't know. Let me ask."

Me: Hey, Sage wants to know who your groomsmen are going to be.

Jason: Blaze, Colt, Hunter, and Mac. I was thinking of asking your brother too.

Me: Oh! You should. I can ask Anna Mae. I don't know her well, but Megan does.

Jason: Let's do it. So, lots of wedding planning?

Me: Yes, I think we're almost there

Jason: Be safe. I love you.

Me: Love you too.

"Okay, he said Blaze, Colt, Hunter, and Mac. Then he said Royce too, so I was thinking we could pair him with Anna Mae? Can we order another dress?"

Riley and Sage share a quick look with a smile. If you blinked, you'd have missed it.

"I'm on it. I'll also text Megan about getting in touch with Anna Mae."

By the time we get to the bridal boutique, the bridesmaids and their dresses are all taken care of.

Chapter 17

Jason

I'm on my way to Blaze's side of the ranch when I get a phone call from the private investigator I hired to check out Seth.

"Tell me you have news," I answer.

"Well, hello to you too. Yes, I was able to lift his prints which linked him as Salvatorio Barak. He spent time in juvie growing up, and his records before he was eighteen are sealed tight. It looks like he was on a good path for a year, started school had good grades, then nothing."

"What do you mean and nothing?"

"There's nothing on him since then. He's a ghost. I'm guessing this is where he started using a new name. I've pulled some contacts, and I have three other identities for him so far in Chicago, Jacksonville, and Boston. Whatever he's into, it's not good if he's jumping around so much. I'm still digging. I just wanted to update you."

I rub my hand down my face and fill him in on how he got Ella's number and tried to call her.

"This guy is great with the nice guy act. My sister was even impressed with how convincing it is. Don't let your guard down around him."

"Okay, just hurry."

"Trust me, I am. This guy doesn't sit well with me. The Sooner I can nail him the better."

We hang up, and I can't help but feel unsettled. I don't like having to send Ella back there, but I don't think I can convince her family to let her stay here either. I have her for a few more days; I have to focus on that.

I spend a few hours in the barn with Blaze and Colt doing inventory. We're getting ready to winter prep the ranch in a few months, and that includes cattle checks.

Nick is running the bar while Ella is in town, so I can get the most time with her. It's just natural to spend time helping my brothers. I love the land even if ranching was never my dream.

Just before lunch, I hear my phone go off and see a text from Ella.

Ella: I found my dress!!
Me: Can I see it?

I know she won't let me, but a man can try, right?

Ella: No, silly, but I've good news!
Me: Hit me with it.
Ella: How would you like to get married in four weeks?

I just walked into Mom and Dad's house for lunch, and the news knocks me over. I have to sit down.

"Jason, you okay?" Dad asks with concern on his face.

"Yeah, just talking to Ella."

Me: Can you and the girls have everything done by then? I'd marry you tomorrow, but I want this wedding to be everything you dreamed of.
Ella: Yep. Just got my dress, and Sage ordered the bridesmaid dresses this morning. Mom is going to do the cake. Your mom is going to do flowers from her garden, and we

can reuse a lot of decorations from your sisters' weddings.

Me: You tell me the date, and I'll be there.

She gives me the date, and I send a text with it out to the guys.

Me: Can you plan everything from Tennessee?

Ella: I have a plan I'll share when I see you tonight.

Me: I can't wait, sweetheart. I love you.

Ella: Love you too.

I take a deep breath and look at Dad, who has a smile on his face.

"So, four weeks," I say.

"Four weeks sounds pretty good to me," Dad agrees.

• • • ● • ● • • •

Ella

We're on our way home from Dallas, and I'm on cloud nine! Not only do I have my wedding dress but in just twenty-four hours, we have half the wedding planned!

Wedding dress shopping was fun, and the girls were right. That place has such a huge selection that it makes finding a dress easy. Of course, the dress I fell in love with wasn't modest enough; it was strapless. I got lucky though. They had another of that same dress they were going to trash because it got ruined in the shop. The sales lady gave it to us, so Mom can use the matching lace to make sleeves for me.

After wedding dress shopping, we went to several stores in Dallas and bought materials to make our own wedding invitations, tons of twinkle lights for the idea I had for the reception, and some of the hair supplies Megan asked us to get.

Don't tell the girls, but I liked the part of shopping for Megan's list the most. It was fun to get hands-on with all the stuff I'll be learning about soon.

Now, we're on our way home, and I've tried to direct the conversation off wedding talk several times. Jason's mom just laughs and winks at me; she knows what I'm doing.

We pull into the ranch, and Jason is just getting out of his truck. He leans against the side and waits for us. My mouth goes dry; he looks so good in his work clothes. He has on Wrangles and a simple gray t-shirt. You can see his brown belt and his belt buckle. Paired with his cowboy boots and cowboy hat, it's a simple outfit, but he wears it well.

"Hey sweetheart, need help carrying anything in?"

"The dress is in a black bag. You can't see it, Jason, and it's going to straight to my room," Sage jokes, and Jason chuckles.

"Well, dinner isn't anything fancy, but we men tried. Maybe after dinner, we can go for a walk?"

"I'd like that."

The guys made simple spaghetti. Noodles and sauce and garlic bread. I love sitting around the table with them. To think, in just four weeks, this will be my everyday routine. It makes me giddy.

"You sure have a big smile on your face," Jason whispers to me.

"Four weeks and this will be my new normal," I whisper back, and a huge smile covers his face as well.

After dinner, Mom and Dad decide to join us on our walk, and we head out.

We walk in silence for a bit, taking in the ranch before Jason speaks.

"So, I was talking to your dad. With the wedding so close and all, we were wondering if you can tie up any loose ends back home in the next two weeks?"

"What do you mean?"

"Can you be ready to move here in two weeks?"

Whoa. I didn't see that coming. I thought we'd come down a few days before the wedding and move my stuff to the house, so it would be ready when we get back from the honeymoon.

"Yeah, I don't have a lot of stuff to pack. That would only take maybe a day. Dad is okay with this?"

"Well, we need you here for wedding planning and your mom. I guess with things going on at church, she has more time than normal. She and Maggie would come with you, bring your stuff, and plan the wedding. Your dad and Royce would join us a few days before the wedding."

"Plus, it gives you time to decorate our room."

"Our room?"

"Well, I thought we'd stay at the main house until we had kids like the others are planning. My room is decorated for me. But it needs your touch. You can unpack your stuff there and redecorate it and get it ready for us when we move in after the honeymoon. I can stay in Colt's old room until then."

"I love decorating! Also, where are we going for our honeymoon?"

"Well, this is the time of year we normally do a family trip to the lake house. I was thinking of taking a page out of Blaze's book and heading up there for a week then inviting everyone up for a week to give you the full family experience. What do you think?"

"I love it!"

"Okay, it's settled. I'll make the plans. I think Nick is excited to have a bit more time to run the place himself. Then the TV special will air two weeks after we get home, so the timing will be great. We should also look at getting you enrolled in classes. I think Megan said the next round starts in two months? If you want to start that soon?"

"This is a lot to plan."

"It is but thankfully, my sisters rock at this, and Mom lives for this. Your soon-to-be husband is a good event planner since he owns an event space in town, you know."

I get those silly butterflies again when he says, 'my soon-to-be husband.' This man is going to be my husband, my first kiss, my first everything. I get to be his wife, and there's nothing that compares to that feeling.

Chapter 18

Jason

We decide to head up to Dallas a day early and rent an Airbnb, so I can spend some time in Dallas with her family. The Dallas Metroplex is so huge and though I grew up an hour away in Rock Springs, it still makes this small-town boy uncomfortable being here. But for my Ella, I'd do anything.

Once we unload our stuff at the Airbnb, we decide to head out and visit the JFK 6th Floor Museum all about the Kennedy assassination. There's a beautiful park nearby too that I want to get some pictures with my girl at.

Ella wants to change out of what she calls her car clothes. When I see her walk out in a simple and casual black dress, my mouth waters. She looks so sexy.

"Ready?" I ask, and she nods.

We spend the day around Dallas, doing all the touristy things they want like the Reunion

Tower with the 360-degree views of the Dallas skyline. We even visit Bonnie and Clyde's gravesites.

After a real Southern dinner, we head back to the Airbnb where Ella heads to her room to do some planning with her mom and Maggie, leaving her dad, Royce, and me in the living room.

Royce gets a phone call and steps out, and I see her dad look at me with that look my dad will give when he has something he wants to talk about.

"Let's hear what's on your mind," I say to get the ball rolling.

"Well, I'm just wondering your thoughts on all this. With her friends dropping Ella because of you, and now people won't let my wife host events she has been doing for over a decade."

"From what I've been told, it's her friends' parents controlling them, so there's no real way to know what they think. I also don't think it matters much since in two weeks, she's moving to Texas where people seem to be a lot more welcoming."

He opens his mouth, but I cut him off. "Let me finish." He nods, so I continue, "I'm sorry that Ella and I courting has brought problems to your family. I really am. But I have my suspicion on where this is rooted and since I can't prove it, I've kept my mouth shut. In all honesty, I think it will die down once Ella moves here, and we're married."

"Why do you say that?"

"I can give you one guess, and it's not a what, it's a who."

Her father thinks for a minute, and I see the moment it crosses his mind. "Seth?"

"Yep. Listen, I've had a private investigator on him, and I don't have anything concrete other than his real name is Salvatorio Barak as per his fingerprints. Salvatorio Barak has ceased to exist since he was nineteen. My guy is still digging, but my guess is whatever he's running from? It's not good."

"Either way, just the fact you're a bar owner is causing tension."

"So who I am doesn't matter? The fact that I'm a business owner who can support myself and provide for my family doesn't matter? The fact that a business I inherited and choose to run and make more family friendly is what everyone is judging me on. I'm sorry for sounding harsh here, but why should I care about them? Are those the type of people your family wants to associate with? I admire you and how you want the best for your family. Maybe you need to think about what that really is."

He's quiet for so long, I'm worried that when he talks, he's going to revoke his permission to marry Ella. Honestly, I don't care if he does. It's happening no matter what.

"I grew up there, and they're good people."

"I'm sure they are. They're also judgmental."

He gives me a half smile. "You always speak your mind?"

"I do; it's a trait I picked up being a *bar owner.* You have to be direct and to the point, because drunks don't get subtle hints. As a business owner, if you aren't direct, people tend to try to walk all over you."

"That I can understand."

"I'm just going to toss something out there and take it for what it is. Maybe it's time for a relocation. Ella is going to be in Rock Springs. It looks like Royce might end up here too. You'll enjoy being closer to your grandkids, and the church here can always use someone like Maria and yourself. Just food for thought."

He nods but doesn't get a chance to speak. The girls pile back into the room.

"I have forced everyone to stop wedding talk for the night. My brain is spinning," Ella says as she comes to sit next to me on the couch.

"Well, you tell me what you need from me, and I'll make it happen," I say.

"Well, we need to know what you plan to wear along with your groomsmen. This is a more casual wedding," Maria says.

"Cowboy formal." I shrug.

"What *is* that exactly?"

"Jeans, a nice shirt and jacket, cowboy boots, and a cowboy hat. Is that okay with you, sweetheart? If you want us in a full tux, we'll do it."

"No, cowboy formal sounds perfect."

"What about in brown?" Maggie says. "It will pair with the bridesmaid dresses perfectly."

"I love that!" Ella says.

"Well, when I get home, I'll get Sage to take a picture. I have a brown formal jacket. Maybe pair it with khakis? We'll have to find what you want for the guys though."

"Gives us something to do at the airport tomorrow," Maggie says.

With that, Ella does stop all wedding talk as we watch some TV.

When I walk my girl and her family into the airport the next morning, I can't seem to shake the feeling that sending her back to Tennessee is a bad idea.

Chapter 19

Ella

I'm nervous because today is the first time I'll be at church since I got engaged. This is the day we tell everyone and since no one likes Jason, my guess is that they won't be too thrilled. I've talked about how I feel to Dad, and he promises that he and Royce won't leave my side today. He also won't let anyone put a damper on this happy day, but I don't tell him it doesn't feel like a happy day.

Don't get me wrong, I'm so excited to marry Jason. I love him with everything that I am. The excitement of being engaged is there when I'm talking to his family and while I was in Texas, but here in Tennessee? Knowing people don't approve, so much so that they've kept my friends from me, just puts a damper on it all.

It makes me want to pack up and move to Texas even sooner and just not deal with everyone here. My room is already half-packed, and I've only been home for four days. The only stuff not packed are my clothes and the stuff on my desk that I'm using for wedding planning.

For the first time in my life, I think about pretending to be sick, so I can get out of going to church. That's just not me. I've always loved to go and be social. I talked to Jason about this last night. He apologized for not being the kind of man I could be proud of at church, and it made me cry.

I told him I couldn't be prouder of him that he was such an amazing man, and that's not what my problem was. I told him I was ashamed of the people I held so dear my whole life and how quickly they turned their backs on me and my family.

We stayed up late talking, and he shocked me by promising to go to church with me as often as I asked him to. I said we'll see how life is out there. I did more church things here just to fill my time. But I plan to fill my time in different ways when I move. He made a comment about keeping me plenty busy then quickly changed the subject.

As I walk into church, I take everything in, and I notice people watch us. This makes me uncomfortable, to say the least. I think the worst with what they're thinking. Dad takes my hand, and we sit. The service takes my mind off everyone, and it seems like we're in our own little bubble in our pew. The second the service is over that bubble breaks.

"Well, there you are, Ella. I didn't see you last week, and when I tried to call your number, it had been disconnected. It seems no one here has your new number," Seth says as he stands a bit too close for my liking.

Dad is right there, stepping between me and Seth, and my brother is right by my side.

"Well, when you weren't given her number to begin with, you have no reason to have it. We won't be updating it at the church, seeing as how Ella will only be a member for a few more weeks," Dad says firmly.

I watch a dark cloud pass over Seth's eyes like he forgot to mask his emotions.

"What do you mean?" he asks, trying to regain his composure.

"Well, we were in Texas last week, and our Ella got engaged. So, she'll be heading down to plan the wedding and moving down there."

"Engaged? To that *bar owner*? He's nothing but trouble. Is that the type of filth you want her to marry? She should be mine, a member of the church. Is she not even going to get married at the church here?" Seth rants, anger evident in his voice.

"Why would I get married here? Everyone has turned their back on me because of Jason."

"Well, I'm sure dumping him and allowing a member of the church such as myself to court you would go along away in repairing your *reputation*."

"Well, she has no interest in you, and neither does my family. I suggest you leave her and us alone," my father snaps at him in that dad voice you only hear when you know you really, really, *really* messed up.

We end up skipping the potluck that day and head home after our confrontation with Seth.

"I can't put my finger on it, but something is off about him," Royce says on our drive home.

"I feel it too. I don't like him," Dad says.

"He just gives me the creeps the way I catch him looking at me. It gives me the chills," I say.

Mom tries to change the subject to a few weddings coming up at church, but the mood never leaves the car until we get home.

• • • • • • • • • •

It's been a few days since our run in at church with Seth and the news has spread quickly about my engagement and I'd be lying if I said people were happy. Many people have called to say how disappointed they are in my dad for allowing me to marry someone like Jason, others have said they think he and my mom should resign their positions in the church.

None of that shocks me as much as when Pastor Will himself shows up to talk to us at home. I am in the kitchen helping my mom make some freezer meals for when she, Maggie, and I head down to Texas next week because Royce and my dad will be staying back for a few days before joining us. We wanted to make sure they ate more than just fast food.

Dad gets the door and joins us in the kitchen. Pastor Will, who has been a friend of the family for many years, looks uncomfortable.

"Grant, Maria, I was hoping to have a word with you," he says.

"Well, I'll head to my room and check my email," I say as I wash my hands.

"Well, maybe you should stay." Pastor Will catches everyone's attention with that.

We settle in the living room. I'm on the couch with Mom on one side and Dad on the other. Pastor Will takes a seat in an armchair across from us.

"There has been a lot of talk around the church, and I don't like to believe rumors, so I wanted to come and hear straight from the source."

"Of course, we'd be happy to answer any questions you have, Pastor. We've always been an open book." Mom smiles at him.

"Well, is it true Ella here is engaged?"

"Yes," I say and hold up my ring to him.

"Can I ask why you haven't been in to see me then?"

"I'm not getting married here. Jason's family owns a large ranch in Texas. On the ranch is a small church his family built over a hundred years ago. It's been a family tradition to get married there, so that's what we're doing with his pastor."

Pastor Will nods. "Well, tell me about your fiancé."

I have a feeling I know where this is going but I still can't help the smile that crosses my face every time I think of Jason.

"He's amazing. His family owns the second biggest ranch in the state of Texas. His parents adopted three kids who needed homes on top of having him, his brother, and his sister. They're all the nicest people you'll ever meet. They'd give you the clothes off their back and a place to stay without a second thought. Jason helps on the ranch, and his siblings and he all live in the house on one side of the ranch. His parents live on the other side."

I take a moment to catch my breath. "He's the oldest kid but never wanted to run the ranch. He's actually a business owner in town and doing well."

"What kind of business?" Pastor Will interrupts me, and I can't help but roll my eyes, which earns me a jab in the side from Dad.

"Well, when he inherited it, it was a small country bar." I watch his disapproval on Pastor Will's face instantly, but I continue, "Since he took it over, he has turned it into an event space that features local talents and is a stop on the Texas concert circuit. He has expanded and turned it into a restaurant. His chef Nick won a BBQ contest in Dallas and now his place is being featured on one of the food TV shows, and he's adding outdoor seating. It's all very family friendly now. He has featured a lot of the history in the area along the walls, showcasing the ranches in the area."

No matter what I say, the disapproval is still on Pastor Will's face like he didn't hear anything I said after the word bar.

"So, the rumors are true. You're letting her marry a bar owner?" he asks Dad.

"What rumors exactly?"

"Well, Seth came to me very concerned about Ella's wellbeing."

"The same Seth who hasn't taken no for an answer, who obtained my phone number from your office without my parents' approval, and forced me to change my phone number. The same Seth who has made veiled threats?" I say with anger in my voice.

"Well yes, but this has all caused quite a stir," Pastor Will starts but this time, it's my turn to interrupt him.

"Funny because the only person who knew about my engagement was Seth since no one else was willing to talk to us after they heard who was courting me. It makes me wonder what exactly people heard and what *Seth* has been saying."

"In light of this news, I think your family should resign any positions in the church..."

Pastor Will starts, but Dad interrupts this time.

"Ella Bear, why don't you head to your room and check those emails. Let me handle this."

I nod and head to my room. The moment my door is closed, I call Jason and between the tears, I tell him what Pastor Will just said.

Chapter 20

Jason

I'm on my way to Tennessee now. I'll drive all night to get there. It seems once Seth got angry, he started to slip up. Ozzy got me everything I need with just two days of following him around.

Ozzy had to turn over everything to the authorities as well, and they're moving to arrest him at this moment.

When my Ella called me crying yesterday about what Pastor Will said, I was fuming. I felt so helpless that there was nothing I could do. I suggested she just finish packing and head down here early and get away from it all. She agreed and has been texting me all day with pictures of her now empty closet and the growing stack of boxes.

Then this morning, Ozzy calls and tells me everything. Within two hours, I was in the car on the way to Ella. She doesn't know I'm coming. I have a few stops on the way, the first being at Ozzy's office to get the folder he has for me.

From what he told me on the phone, it's not pretty. Things my Ella doesn't need to ever know about if I can help it.

On the drive, I try to keep calm and distract myself. Sage said to crank up some music, so that's what I do all the way through Arkansas. Once I reach the Tennessee state border, I can't seem to keep the nerves away until I reach Ozzy's office.

I head in and knock on his office door since there's no receptionist at the desk.

"Ozzy?" I ask.

"Ahh, that sounds like Jason."

"Nice to meet you in person."

"Same here. I wish it were under better circumstances."

"So do I. Any updates?"

"Well, the local authorities arrested Seth, and he'll be held until he can get in front of a judge to set bail."

"Any idea when that will be?"

"Could be in as little as forty-eight hours or as long as a week. I just don't know. Once bail is set, he would have to pay it. So, my best advice is to get Ella out of here sooner rather than later."

"That's the plan, but I have one more stop."

He hands me the folder and shakes my hand. "I'll keep my eye on him and let you know if he makes bail."

"Sounds good."

I head out to my car and look at the folder. What I see makes my stomach roll, so I put it down and head to my next stop.

It's a short drive and to say I'm dreading this talk is to say the least. I head to the church that has been so close to Ella and her family for many years and head into the office.

"Hello, I'm hoping to speak to Pastor Will," I tell the lady at the front desk.

"Do you have an appointment?" she asks sweetly.

"No, but if you could tell him it's urgent and about Ella Stevenson?"

I watch concern on her face. "Is she okay?"

"I don't want to come off rude, but maybe you should call and ask her. Too many people here have turned their backs on that family recently and what I have in this folder will prove you were all lied to. Now please, Pastor Will."

I watch the color drain from her face as she disappears to an office in the back. A moment later, a gentleman in his forties follows her out and walks up to me.

"I'm Pastor Will. I understand you wish to speak to me?"

"Yes, it's urgent and a delicate situation. If we can speak in private?"

"Of course, right this way. I'm sorry I didn't get your name?"

"I'm Jason Buchanan, Ella's fiancé," I say as he closes the door. I watch his demeanor change. So I keep talking. "I'm aware of the conversation you had with her family yesterday, and I have some information here you need to be aware of," I say and hold up the folder.

"Seeing how the whole church has passed judgment on Ella's family and myself on the word of a Seth Covine, I'm sure you've heard he was just arrested?"

Will's face pales just a bit. "No, I was unaware."

"Of course, since his name isn't Seth Covine. The name he used last year was Alexander Daniels. The year before that? Maddix Garrett. Before that? Jordan Bovine. His legal name is Salvatorio Barak. He has a juvie record over a mile long and many warrants out for his arrest across several states." I hand him the folder.

"Be warned what you'll find in there isn't pretty. We can start with just the last forty-eight hours, there are photos of him drinking at a local bar and snorting cocaine, and having sex three different times, with three different women in the backseat of his car. He has multiple rape charges, and several women he has associated with over the last few years have disappeared. He would change his name and move on before he could be questioned."

My phone goes off with a text, so I let all that sink in.

Ozzy: Doesn't look like he'll be making bail. Charges are still coming in.

Me: Thanks. Keep me updated.

"That was my private investigator. It looks like he won't be making bail. So now I ask, what made you or anyone at this church trust the word of one man who had been here not more than a few months over the word and decisions of a family who has been at this church for almost thirty years? Which, according to my research, is longer than *you've* been."

"He was rather convincing, saying he has talked with Ella..."

I interrupt, "He harassed Ella. If you had been bothered to ask, he followed her and wouldn't take no for an answer or leave her alone when asked. She had to have her father step in many times."

"I was unaware."

"Until yesterday, you never once talked to the family to get their side. I was here at this very church when I was in town, and not one person came up to get to know me or ask if what they heard was true. You all heard one word, bar, and passed judgment on me. I attend church and even I know there's only one man who can judge me. If I remember correctly, His son had meals with whores."

With that, I stand and pick up the folder that has been left on Will's desk.

"I love Ella with everything I am, and I'll give her anything she wants. She was heartbroken that this church turned its back on her the way it did."

With that, I turn and head out the door, not looking back. My next stop is to get my Ella in my arms. Even knowing Seth, or whatever his name is, is behind bars, I still won't be able to keep calm until I see with my own eyes that she's okay.

The drive to her house from the church is short, but it seems to take forever. I pull in, and the house is missing the buzz of life that it had the last time I was here. I grab the folder and knock on the front door.

Grant answers with a surprised look on his face. I try to force a smile.

"We need to talk, but I need to see Ella first."

He nods and opens the door. Ella is sitting on the couch in the living room watching TV. As soon as she sees me, she jumps up and runs into my arms. I hold her tight and swing her around, relieved.

"Jason! What are you doing here?" I can hear the excitement in her voice, and I wish it were under better circumstances. I don't want that darkness to dampen her light, so I set her down and rest my forehead on hers for just a moment to gain my composure before kissing the top of her head and stepping back.

"Well, I need to talk to your dad first, okay?"

"Everything okay?"

"Everything is perfect now. I promise we'll talk, okay?"

She nods, and I pull her in for a hug one more time, pushing my luck before I follow her dad into his study. I close the door and sit.

"I'm assuming this is about Pastor Will's visit yesterday? I know Ella called you."

I hand him the folder, and he slides on his reading glasses to go over it as I relay everything to him from hiring a private investigator, to what he found, what I told Pastor Will, and the last text from Ozzy.

"I don't see him making bail, but I think you and your family shouldn't be here in case he does."

He sets the folder down and looks me over.

"Let me ask you this. What made you hire a private investigator?"

"Something with Seth's story didn't sit right with me. I didn't like what Ella told me about her encounters with him. My parents always say to go with your gut. If I were overreacting and nothing came up, so be it. Ella and I could have a good laugh about it down the road. But on the off chance, I was right? I needed to protect not just Ella but you guys too. I knew even back then you would be my family one day."

He removes his glasses and taps them on his chin before he smiles.

"Knowing you would go to this length to make sure Ella is okay is what any father would hope for." He stands, so I do too. "I agree. I think we should head out to Texas tomorrow if that's okay?"

"Of course, I'd suggest staying through the wedding. Maybe a week after as a small vacation?"

"I like the sound of that. Nothing is holding us here as of yesterday, and any work I need to do can be done online."

"Sir, one thing."

"I think you've earned the right to call me Grant, or Dad, at this point."

I smile. "Grant, if we could not tell Ella the gory details on Seth. I don't want her to worry about how much trouble she might have been in since he's now behind bars."

"I agree, but she needs to know it's serious."

"I agree with that."

"Well, let's get everyone packing and give Ella the good news."

Chapter 21

Ella

We just crossed the Texas state line. I'm riding in Jason's truck with Mom. After Jason talked with Dad yesterday, Dad asked if I wanted to head to Texas now. Everyone agreed, and it was a mad rush to get finished packing. All my stuff fit in Jason's truck and my parents' SUV since I didn't need to bring any furniture.

At dinner, Dad and Jason told us about Seth, or Salvatorio I guess is his name, but I still think of him as Seth. Knowing Jason went to such lengths to make sure not only I was safe, but my family, warmed my heart. To know he went to Pastor Will and not only stuck up for me, but for my parents, made me fall in love with him all over again.

As we cross into Texas, I see Jason visibly relax, and I get this sense of home that I haven't had in Tennessee for many weeks. I know then that I'm where I'm meant to be.

"So, does your family know we're coming early?" I ask.

Jason glances over at me for a second before his eyes are on the road. He gives me a half smile and squeezes my hand. "Our family, sweetheart. Our family. And yes I called Sage last night, so she could have your rooms ready. She said she would tell everyone. The girls are excited because it will make wedding planning easier."

"I agree. Sage said the bridesmaid dresses are in, so we need to do a fitting tomorrow and see how much tailoring needs to be done," Mom says. "I also want to do a dress fitting on you again and see how it's coming along."

"And where will this dress fitting be held?" Jason asks with a mischievous glint in his eyes and a smile on his face.

"In a room with the shades drawn and the door locked. You won't see that dress until she's walking down the aisle," Mom jokes right back with him.

Time flies as we head toward Rock Springs, but Mom's phone keeps going off. After what must be the tenth ping, I turn in my seat to look at her.

"Who is blowing up your phone? I know it's not Daddy because he's driving."

"It's nothing." I can tell Mom is a bit annoyed.

"Mom, I'm not a kid anymore. You're always there for me to share my problems. Let me do the same for you."

She sighs and smiles at me. "It's people from church asking me to take events back over and step back into my role like nothing happened."

"What have you told them?" I ask.

"Nothing. I don't know how I feel about all this. Plus, it will be several weeks before we're back in Tennessee anyway."

"Want my opinion for what it's worth?" I ask.

"Always, Ella Bear."

"I think you should tell them you're planning your daughter's wedding and won't be available for the next month. Then over the next month, think about how you feel. If they can turn their back on you so fast like that, then they aren't true friends. I have no interest in reconnecting with the girls in Tennessee. None of them have my new number anyway."

"How did you become so smart?" Mom asks.

"I learned from you." I smile back at her.

The moment we pull up at the ranch, the girls all come running out and surround me in a huge group hug.

"Welcome home," Sage says with the biggest smile on her face.

"Come on, let's feed them. They've been driving all day!" Megan says and laughs.

"I have a full schedule planned for all things wedding related, so we get everything done," Riley chimes in.

"Since she has become pregnant, she has developed these organizational freak tendencies," Sage whispers.

"I heard that!" Riley sing songs.

"And supersonic hearing," Sage whispers again, causing everyone to laugh.

When we head inside, Jason's mom is there and hugs me too. The guys all file out and unload the boxes.

"Where do you want it?" Mac asks.

"Anything labeled clothes into the guest room where Ella is staying. Everything else into my room," Jason says and then he looks at my parents. "I'm going to stay in Colt's old room until the wedding, so Ella can get a chance to fix our room up how she wants."

Dad looks at me. "Maybe you'll want your own place?"

"Oh, we'll be picking out a cabin on the ranch and start renovations on it. Most of them need to be fixed up, and some haven't been used in a few decades. I want Ella to pick the place, and we can make it our own. The room is just while renovations are underway, but I still want her to make it a home for us."

I smile then and turn to Riley. "Come upstairs with me, and let's go over the schedule while I unpack some clothes."

Once up in my room, I close my door.

"I need a favor." I turn to Riley.

"Ohh, a super-secret mission! I love it. Hit me with it."

"I want you to schedule a time you, me, Sage, and Megan can go shopping just the four of us. No moms, no guys, no chaperones, just us four. Call it a sister bonding trip. A day of shopping in Dallas."

"I can do that. What are we shopping for?"

"It's a surprise." I wink at her, and she laughs.

"I'm on it!"

She then fills me in on all things wedding planning while I hang up my clothes. When Jason called last night, they moved some things around, so the schedule wasn't so rushed. Tomorrow, we meet with Pastor Greg to go over the wedding service.

I guess he's loving being able to do the weddings in the old church, so he agreed. But he wants to meet with Jason and me first. There are some meetings for food, fittings, shopping, décor planning, and DIY sessions all scheduled in.

Even with the mountain of work ahead of us, I couldn't be happier.

· · · ● · ● ● · · ·

I've been home in Rock Springs for a few days now, and today is our sister shopping trip into Dallas. Mom and Dad thought it was a great idea to have some bonding time with my future sisters. If they only knew the alternate agenda, they might disown me.

"Okay, so what is the plan today other than shopping in Dallas?" Riley asks.

I smile. "Well, I need your help, and it needs to stay a secret."

"It's not illegal, is it? Cause I'm totally down, but give a girl a head's up and all," Sage jokes. But part of me knows she isn't joking; family is important to her, and she'd do anything for them.

"No, it's just not something my parents would approve of, I don't think." I blush. And Megan, who's in the backseat with me, takes my hand.

"Lay it on us," she says.

"Well, I need some clothes for the honeymoon."

"You're going to the lake house, right? What type of clothes, like shorts and a swimsuit?"

"To start with and ummm... nighttime clothes and uhh... something for under my wedding dress."

The car goes silent, and I know my face must be bright red and even more so when all eyes are on me.

"Like make him swallow his tongue and lose his shit, sexy stuff for under the wedding dress?" Riley finally asks.

I nod, and they all let out happy whoops and hollers, causing me to laugh.

"I can hide them in my room since you'll get ready in there," Sage says, which causes me to smile. "But if I'm being honest, I don't think you have to go too over the top to make him lose control. Just being able to touch you will do it."

"Yeah, there's something about men seeing you in your wedding dress on the wedding night. That alone is enough," Megan adds.

"Well, we'll make that our first stop. Do you still want some new clothes or a bathing suit?"

"Well, I was thinking for a bathing suit, a one-piece with some shorts like the old pin-up models? Something modest still but better than what I have now."

"This is going to be so much fun. She's like a life-size Barbie!" Megan squeals, making us all laugh.

"I take it you had the biggest Barbie collection growing up?" I ask.

"Heck yes, I did. How do you think I got into doing hair?"

We all laugh, and the feeling of home and family wash over me.

The girls take me to a classy and fun lingerie shop, and the sales lady is helpful. I get the perfect white, what they call a baby doll for under my wedding dress. Sage insists on buying it since they can't give me a proper bridal shower and gift me these items in front of my parents.

Riley and Megan both buy me an outfit as well.

"So, I have a confession," Sage says.

"Uh oh," Megan jokes and laughs.

"When Jason heard we were going shopping, he gave me his credit card for you, Ella. He said to buy whatever you wanted: clothes, décor, makeup, whatever. He made me swear not to bring you home until you did."

I shake my head. "I can't spend his money."

Sage holds her hand up. "Take it up with him."

As we head back to the car to go on to the next shop, I pull out my phone and call Jason.

"I was waiting for this call, sweetheart." He greets me, and I can hear the smile on his face.

"I don't want to spend your money, Jason."

"Ella sweetheart, it is my privilege and my joy to be able to spoil you. I want to give you everything you want or need. This is just the beginning. Let me do this for you, please."

With logic like that, I can't tell him no, and he knows it.

"Okay, I'll pick up a few things."

"Thank you, sweetheart. You girls having fun?"

"Yeah, we're heading to lunch now. Then a bit more shopping before we head back."

"Okay, be safe. I'll see you at dinner. I love you, Ella."

"I love you too, Jason."

After lunch, we hit the mall, and I grab a few new outfits, including a pair of shorts, my first ever, and a few pairs of jeans, also my first ever. I get a few flannel shirts for around the ranch, and I end up finding the bathing suit I wanted, and I love it.

We wander around the mall, and I pick up a few photo frames for our room as well to hold wedding photos.

Our room.

I like the sound of that.

Chapter 22

Jason

The day after tomorrow, I get to marry the love of my life. Today, the guys and I are cleaning up the ranch church. It's in good shape from Sage and Megan's weddings, but we're still giving it the once over on order from the girls.

"I think they just wanted to get us out of the house," Colt grumbles.

"I agree. This list is busy work. Clean the pews, wax the floors, dust, make sure windows are streak free. Come on."

"You think that's bad, Riley just texted me and said we should rotate the pews," Blaze says.

"What the hell does that mean?" I ask.

"They want the pews from the front moved to the back and the ones in the back moved to the front," he replies.

"How the hell will they know?" Mac asks.

"I don't know, but you know they will. It's just busy work. Maybe I can get out of it if I promise to take you all into town for the day." Blaze pulls out his phone and starts rapid fire texting Riley.

The rest of us sit down and wait for him to finish.

"You ready for this?" Hunter nods toward the front of the church.

"Were you?" I ask.

He laughs and looks at his feet. "Yeah, but then again, I had been trying to get your sister down the aisle for five years before she agreed. Then I couldn't get it done fast enough. Didn't want her changing her mind and all."

I laugh. Megan and Hunter met when they were sixteen, but she friend-zoned him until a few months back, just after Blaze's wedding. I can't blame the guy for wanting to lock her down quickly after all that time.

"I've been waiting my whole life for Ella. I just didn't know it. Then one day, there she is, and everything fell into place. Like you, I can't get her down the aisle fast enough."

I stare at the front of the church, trying to picture us up there in about forty-eight hours. I can't wipe the smile off my face. Forty-eight hours, and we'll have our first kiss. She'll be mine, no more chaperones.

I've been trying too hard to keep my mind off the wedding night. Just the mere thought of it makes my cock painfully hard. I can't wait to get her alone and take my time with her. It's not even about the sex. Okay, it's not just about the sex, but it's about falling asleep with her in my arms and waking up with her there too. It's about being able to kiss her anytime I want and starting our life together. No more chaperones.

But it's also about the sex. Being able to slowly slide that wedding dress off her and run my hands down her sides...

"Okay, Riley admitted it was busy work and said we could head into town as long as we didn't come back until she gave the all clear," Blaze interrupts my thoughts.

I have to shift to find a more comfortable position. My cock pressing against my zipper reminds me how close we are to having our Ella all to ourselves.

"All right, let's go," Colt says as we all head out to Blaze's truck and pile in.

"Blaze, did you think this through? What are we going to do in town for the next several hours?" I ask.

"Hang out at my parents' place, Mom just put a batch of wings in the oven," Hunter says.

His mom is a good cook, and she has become like family since Hunter and Megan have started hanging out and even more so since they got married.

We're pulling into his parents' driveway when Ozzy calls me.

"Why don't you guys head in. I have to take this," I tell them before I answer.

"Hey, Ozzy."

"Jason, I'll get to the point. Somehow, Seth made bail."

"What? I thought he has warrants for his arrest."

"He does, but they have to prove it's him first. The judge I think was paid off because he set a bond for him. A high one, but he still paid it."

"Well, at least I got Ella out of there."

"That's the thing, Jason. He has disappeared again, but the people he was in the jail with kept saying he was talking about heading to Texas."

My blood runs cold. If he's heading here, it could mean trouble. Being the second biggest ranch in the state means it would just take an internet search to locate us. It's a little harder to nail down the exact location of the ranch since all mailing addresses are in town, but it's possible.

"We get married the day after tomorrow," I tell him.

"My guess is he wants to try to stop that. I'd alert the local sheriff and have some extra security on the ranch and at the wedding."

"All right. Thanks for the head's up."

"Any time. I'm still keeping an ear to the ground on him, but my guess is he sees Ella as the one who got away."

"She was never his to begin with, but I see where you're coming from."

After I hang up, I take a few deep breaths then call the sheriff to fill him in on everything that has happened with Seth.

"Jason, you know I'll be at the wedding. I guess I'll just make sure to have my badge and my gun as well."

"Thanks, Sheriff. I'm going to talk to the family now and make some plans."

"See you soon, Jason. Call me if you need anything."

I take a few deep breaths then head inside to break the bad news to the guys. I find them all chowing down on chicken wings, but my stomach is rolling too much to think about eating.

Colt wipes his hand and mouth. "What's wrong, Jason?"

"Remember the private investigator I hired to track that Seth guy?"

They all nod.

"He called. Somehow, Seth made bail and now he has disappeared. Ozzy did some digging and found out he was talking about needing to get to Texas."

Colt pulls out his phone. "Let me call Sage and have her put the ranch on lockdown."

"Mac, if you could pick a girl without some drama, that would be great," Blaze jokes and Mac shakes his head.

"Nah, it's the bachelor life for me. I'm too young for all this."

"Okay, she's on it. She's going to call Mom and Dad to get them involved," Colt says.

"I talked to the sheriff. He'll be at the wedding on duty but still as a guest. He's getting the info from the police in Tennessee now."

"Why don't I get some of the guys from the reservation to come out. They'll look like guests but can be on the watch for him."

"Do it. I'll cover all costs for any clothes they need. Khakis, a button-down shirt, and boots will fit right in."

He steps outside to make the phone call.

"Maybe we should head back to the ranch, even if we just hang out at Mom and Dad's. I'd feel better if we were closer," I suggest.

"I know that feeling, and I won't argue with it. Let me text Riley, and we can head out," Blaze agrees.

"Get us a picture of this Seth guy, so we can help be on the lookout as well," Hunter's dad says.

"Thanks." I hug them both before we make our way out to the truck.

On the way back to the ranch, Mac confirms he has guys who are willing to come out if we feed them. It's a small price to pay for my girl's safety. I won't let anyone ruin this day for her. She'll be mine, she'll have the wedding of her dreams, and the wedding night of mine.

I'll do anything to make sure of that.

Anything.

Chapter 23

Ella

I can tell something is going on. Everyone seems tenser, especially Jason. And it's not just that the wedding is tomorrow tense. I've asked a few people what's going on, and they all just smile and say there's a lot to do before the wedding, but I know better.

Talk at dinner tonight is small talk; it isn't anything meaningful, but I can tell they're avoiding something.

Maybe it's nothing, and my mind has gotten the better of me or maybe something is going on they are all hiding from me and I aim to find out what it is. I won't have it hanging over my head on my wedding day.

Everyone went to bed about an hour ago, so now I'm going to do something stupid, but I need to put my mind at ease. I sneak down the hall to the family bedrooms in the east wing. I know which one Jason is staying in, and it's easy to make my way there. The doors along the hall are all closed.

I reach the door to Colt's old room and don't even bother knocking. I hear the soft sounds of a TV on the other side, so I quietly open the door and slip in, closing it behind me. Jason must hear the sound because he sits up in bed.

"Ella, what the hell are you doing here?" he asks with concern all over his face.

"I need to talk to you."

"This couldn't have been done on the phone? This isn't a good idea for you to be in here."

That's when I notice Jason doesn't have a shirt on, and I can see the top of his boxer briefs, letting me know that's all he has on. He has that perfect tan chest and hard muscles and abs from the ranch work. The kind of muscles you can't get in a gym, the kind you only get from hard manual labor.

I have to rub my thighs together. Just seeing him like this is doing things to my body I can't think about right now. We need to talk. He pulls the blanket over himself and growls at me.

"Ella, you need to stop looking at me like that."

My eyes snap back to his, and his eyes bore into me. Why did I come in here again? Oh right, to find out what's going on.

"I know everyone is stressed, Jason, but it's more than normal before the wedding stress, and no one will tell me what's going on, so I have to ask you."

"Ella, it's exactly what they say, pre-wedding stress."

"Do you not trust me, Jason?" I watch hurt cross his face. "I'm going to be your wife tomorrow, and you can't tell me what's going on?"

"I have it handled. I want you to enjoy our wedding day tomorrow."

I hate to do this and hope he won't call my bluff, but I won't have him start our marriage off by keeping things from me.

"There will be no wedding day if you don't tell me what the devil is going on! I won't start our marriage off by you withholding stuff from me. I won't do it, Jason," I raise my voice.

That's when I see the anger hit him, and he stands, confirming my earlier thoughts of him being in only boxer briefs. The impressive bulge in them has me swallowing hard. My mouth is suddenly dry. I watch him take a few steps toward me.

"You telling me you won't marry me over this?"

"Yes, Jason. I won't have you keeping stuff from me. We're in this together, good or bad, and if it's big enough that everyone else knows but you all are keeping it from me? That's something I won't have." I cross my arms and steel my face the best I can.

I watch him look over my face a few times before he sighs and runs his hand through his hair and sits on the edge of the bed.

"The private investigator called, the one who was looking into Seth for me. Somehow, Seth made bail and then he disappeared. He had been saying that he needed to get to Texas. We think he's coming after you based on his... history."

Well, this wasn't what I was expecting, so I take a deep breath. On shaky legs, I walk over and stand in front of him. I know I shouldn't be here. I know I should turn around and head back to my room. But this man will be my husband in less than twenty-four hours, and I'll be expected to be in his bed, so what's wrong with a few more minutes.

I take a few steps closer to him, and I see him grip the sheets on the bed next to him like he's trying to stop himself from reaching for me. I watch his breathing pick up like mine does as I reach out a hand to slowly lay it on his chest over his heart.

I can feel his heart racing as fast as mine. He doesn't say a word as my hand slowly moves down to the center of those first set of perfect abs. I can see the outline of his hard cock through his boxer briefs, and it gives me a slight thrill to know I'm the cause of that.

He swallows hard then reaches out and grabs my hand and brings it to his mouth, placing a kiss inside my palm. His eyes meet mine, and I bring my other hand up to his face. He closes his eyes for just a brief second, soaking in my touch before he opens them and finds my eyes again.

"Ella sweetheart, you have to go back to your room. I want you so damn much, but we've made it this long. Just twenty-four more hours, I promise it will be worth it. I need you to be the strong one right now and turn around and walk out that door. Please, sweetheart, please." He barely whispers the last part.

I know he's right. I take a deep breath, nod, and take a few steps back. I take one more long look at him before I turn and walk toward the door. Having just a little bit more fun with him, I add a little extra sway in my hips, and I'm rewarded with a low groan from him.

When I reach the door, I look back over my shoulder, and he hasn't moved, not one inch.

"I love you, Jason. Thank you for telling me the truth."

His whole face softens. "I love you too, Ella, and will protect you, always. Tomorrow will be perfect, just wait and see."

I smile. "I know it will. You wouldn't let it be any other way."

I let my eyes run over his body one last time, committing it to memory. Before I turn to head out the door, I hear him whisper in that gruff voice.

"Ella?"

"Yes?"

"How wet are you right now?"

I'm taken back by his question but with everything that has happened in the last few minutes, I decide to be brave. I give him a playful smile.

"Soaked."

He groans as I open the door and close it behind me. The hall is still dark, and the house quiet as I make my way back to my room.

· · · · ● · ● · · · ·

I'm getting married today. Tonight, I won't have to leave Jason's room. I haven't spoken a word about last night to anyone, but I had such a hard time falling asleep. All I wanted was to sneak back down the hall and fall asleep in his arms.

Sage and Megan have just helped me into my dress, so Mom and my sister won't see Jason's surprise I have under it. I know they won't approve even though the wedding night is all about sex. It's just not talked about openly in our lives. I know that will change for me once I'm married, and I can't wait.

The things Jason makes me feel are like a rollercoaster ride filled with more highs and stomach-dropping exciting moments than lows. I can't wait to see where it takes me next.

We're getting ready in Sage's room. It's a tradition Riley started, and they've continued. Megan is doing my hair and makeup, and it's just been fun having them all here with Anna Mae, Jason's mom, and Mom.

"It's been a long time since I've had a fun girls get together like this," I say, looking around the room.

"We have girls nights where we kick the boys out of the house, but it has been a while. We'll have to do one when you get back," Sage says.

"I'd like that."

"Where are you going on your honeymoon?" Helen, Jason's mom asks.

"Well, tonight, we're staying at a cabin. Tomorrow we head out to the lake house."

"Oh, I thought you were just meeting us there next week. I didn't know you would be there this week too. You'll love it. It's such a small town, we always have so much fun. You'll see when the family shows up. No ranch work, just bonding time."

"Some of my best memories are at the lake house," Sage says with a smile, and Megan agrees.

"All right, come here. Let me get one more look at the dress," Mom says.

The dress was originally strapless but because of the extra lace we got from the ruined dress at the store my Mom raised the neckline of the dress and gave it long lace sleeves that still show plenty of skin. It's not big and poufy like a lot of wedding gowns are, and there's no tulle in it. The top is form-fitting and has a wrapped fabric look, then the bottom has ruffles made of lace. It has a vintage feel to it that I just love.

Sage's phone goes off, and she announces, "Okay, the guys are at the church. Let's head outside and get you on the horse for some pictures."

I had this idea to ride over to the church in my dress on a horse. I saw a photo on a wedding website about it. When I showed the girls, they loved it too. There was something about being up on the horse, wild and free with the wedding dress on display that spoke to me.

I showed the picture to Jason, and he loved the idea. He wants to frame it in our room and later have it hanging in our living room. He even asked about having it at the bar, which for some reason, I liked the thought of him having a piece of me there with him.

We have fun with the pre-wedding photos with me and the girls and then on the horse. As we finish photos, everyone's phones but mine goes off. I know it's not good when they all look at each other, then at me.

Chapter 24

Jason

I've been at my parents' house all day as the girls get ready in Sage's room. Today is my wedding day, and we're still a few hours away from Ella walking down the aisle to me. My nerves are getting the best of me. Not because I'm nervous to marry Ella, but for all the waiting that still has to happen before I do.

"Why don't you go for a walk?" Mom says, breaking my thoughts.

"Yeah, I guess I can head down to the church to see if they need any help."

"That's a good idea. You need to be doing something; sitting here will only make time drag."

I give Mom a kiss on her cheek and walk down what used to be the old driveaway to my parents' house. It passes right by the church. Once we bought Sage's property, we combined the driveways, and they split once you are on the property, so the church is now more secluded.

As I walk, I can't help but think of when Ella snuck into my room last night. I haven't told anyone. I like having that little secret between us. It kept me awake and hard most of the night. I ended up trying to relive the pain and get my cock to soften three times before I gave up. He wasn't happy with my hand knowing he gets the real thing tonight.

With that thought alone, he's back at attention, making things uncomfortable. I try to adjust myself, but it's no help.

As I near the church, the ranch comes to life. I hear the buzz of people moving around and cars coming and going long before I can set my eyes on the church. When I round the corner, what I see brings a huge smile on my face. My family and friends are all working to put the church together just as my girl asked, and I know there's another group of people at the event barn working there. She has asked me not to peek there. It's a surprise. It has me intrigued, but I'd give her anything, so I'll do as she asks.

Mac sees me walk up first and smiles.

"Couldn't stay away?" he asks.

"I need something to do. Please put me to work," I beg.

"I was the same way. Time moved so slow." Colt joins us.

"We just finished cleaning up the outside a bit and have been directed to hang flowers if you want to help," Mac offers.

As I walk toward the church, I get this prickling feeling on the back of my neck. The one you get when someone is watching you. It has me unsettled. I stop, turn, and take in everyone that's outside the church. I see several of Mac's friends from the reservation, the girls from Megan's hair salon who are overseeing the flowers in the church, and one of the police officers I know is here undercover, a friend of Dad's.

I scan the tree line because this feeling isn't going away but I don't see anything. I head inside the church and look around. People from inside are moving in and out, and I spot Mac and Colt helping with some flowers at the end of the pews. There's a guy at the front of the church with his back to me. There's something familiar about him, but something unsettling too.

I catch Colt's eye and nod my head toward the guy. Without a word, he looks and shrugs.

I hope I'm just overreacting, but I make my way up to the aisle and clear my throat when I'm near him.

When the man turns around, I know instantly why he is familiar and why I'm unsettled around him. The eyes staring back at me are Seth's.

"Well, if it isn't the happy groom who stole my girl?" Seth sneers at me.

This catches Mac and Colt's attention, and I know they're thinking about how to get the girls in the church to safety and take Seth down at the same time. My job is to keep Seth's attention.

"What are you doing here, Seth?" I ask and slowly move to stand to his side, so he has to turn his attention away from the door.

"I came for Ella, of course. She's too good to marry a *bar owner*. I don't know what her father was thinking, but then I realized you probably paid the old man off for her. So, I'm here to double whatever you paid him, and bam, wedding over."

I shift a bit more and out of the corner of my eye, I see Mac moving the girls out of the church. Colt hasn't moved; he's there for back up, but I hope Mac is heading to get the sheriff.

"I didn't pay him off, Seth. Ella isn't someone who can be bought. She chose me."

"No, she was meant to be mine!" He raises his voice, and I see his bloodshot eyes and get a whiff of what I'm sure is scotch on his breath. His hair is ruffled, and I now know he's not thinking logically. His next move is a wild card.

"What about all those other girls, Seth?" I ask, trying to buy some time.

"They meant nothing! They couldn't even rival Ella. She's pure, and I've never had a virgin." He closes his eyes and licks his lips. My stomach rolls at the thought of him putting his hands on my beautiful angel.

He opens his eyes and continues, "They were crack whores who would do anything for their next hit. No one will miss them." He waves his hand in the air like he believes he could do what he wanted with them.

"That's where you're wrong. The police have been looking for them and have found the bodies of half of the girls they connected you to. That's how come I don't understand how you were able to get a bail set."

Seth smiles. "You like that? It's always good to know who the dirty cops and lawmen are in the city. You pad their pockets, scratch their back, and help them out, so when you need help, they have no choice but to help you. You know just enough of their secrets that they're too scared not to."

He smiles and shakes his head before continuing, "The good ole judge has a little drug habit and needed to discreetly get his fix. I arranged that, so can you imagine if he didn't help me, what would happen."

I see Mac enter the church with the sheriff, the undercover cop I saw earlier today, and a few of Mac's friends from the reservation. They're all quiet, and the sheriff holds his finger to his mouth, not wanting me to draw attention to them.

"So, what's your plan if Ella won't go with you and if her father doesn't agree?"

"Oh, Ella will go with me. She'll want to save you. Manipulating her won't be hard. Her father does seem to be a bit smarter. He's so damn clean, I couldn't dig up anything on him, so I had a few things manufactured." He taps his coat pocket.

"Like what?"

"Some photos of him with drugs and women, all the stuff that will ruin his marriage and get him banned from the church."

"But the church knows about you, as does his wife. Why would they believe you now?"

Seth raises his chin and looks at me. "What they know is I was arrested and wrongly accused. That's why I was let out."

"No, Seth, how do you think the law found you?" I ask and watch his wheels turn. "I had a PI on you. I know your last five aliases, and I turned you over. I showed it all to the church and Ella's parents."

In a split second, he reaches for his gun I caught a glimpse of earlier, but the alcohol has made him slow and unsteady, and I'm faster.

I grab the arm reaching for his gun and use the momentum to spin him and face plant him on the ground before he realizes what's going on.

"You son of a bitch, get off me!" Seth yells as he struggles to break free from my grasp and fails.

The sheriff runs up, holsters his gun, and pulls out his handcuffs.

"I got him, Jason," he says and takes over, reading him his rights.

"One more thing, *Seth*," the undercover cop says as he walks up, "We don't take kindly to people who think they can work the system with dirty cops here. We have a special cell just for you."

Seth spits in his face, and the cop laughs as he wipes his face clean.

"By Texas law, that qualifies as assaulting an officer. You're going to be a fun one," the cop says.

Seth doesn't seem to want to go easily and struggles with every step. I follow them outside where they take him to the unmarked car parked on the side of the church.

"I'll take him in. You stay and enjoy the wedding. I think I'm going to have fun locking him in cell C," the undercover cop says to the sheriff.

They share a few words as Colt comes up to me. "What do you want to tell the girls?"

"The truth. Why don't you send a group text out, let everyone know at once? Leave Ella out of it. I'm going to call her and tell her myself."

Colt nods, and I see him pull out his phone and text as I watch Seth being hauled away. I turn to Jill, one of the girls helping from Megan's shop.

"You girls okay?"

"Yeah, is it okay to get back in there and see what needs to be fixed up?" she says.

"Yep, you're good to go. I don't think much will need to be fixed up."

I feel my phone go off in my pocket as Colt looks up at me and nods.

I walk away from the crowd a bit and call Ella.

"Jason, what the devil is going on?"

"Ella sweetheart, everything is okay. Seth showed up, but he wasn't too smart. We got him handled, and he's on his way to jail now. No one was hurt, except Seth."

"What?! He really showed up? What did he want? Where was he? Are you sure you're okay?"

I chuckle. "Slow down, sweetheart. Yes, I'm fine. Colt and Mac were there. They can tell you the same thing, not a scratch on me. It happened at the church. I came out here for a walk, and I'm glad I did."

"Oh no, the church. Did he mess it up too bad?"

"No, sweetheart. Jill is in there now. Let me ask her."

"Yes, please."

I walk towards Jill, who is coming out of the church.

"Ella wants to know how bad the decorations are messed up."

"Only one arrangement needs to be fixed. We're set to go as scheduled."

"Hear that? I'll see you in in fifty-eight minutes, I'll be the one at the end of the aisle," I try to joke.

"Oh, Jason." I can hear the smile in her voice. "I'll be the one in white."

Chapter 25

Ella

I can't believe Seth showed up on my wedding day. Okay, yes, I can believe it. He's just that horrible.

"Well, at least you'll have a good story to tell about the wedding when your kids are older," Sage tries to joke. I give her a halfhearted smile.

It's time to make our way to the church, and I'm a ball of nerves. I'm excited to marry Jason, but part of me is wondering what else will go wrong. Another part of me is nervous as hell for our first kiss. Who has their first kiss in front of everyone they know? Why didn't I think this through earlier?

Just before we make our way to the church, I grab my phone and text Jason, hoping he'll answer.

Me: I don't want our first kiss to be in front of everyone! What were we thinking!

Jason: Then it won't be. Trust me?

Me: Always.

Jason: See you soon, sweetheart.

Deep breaths and just trust Jason. That's all I need to do. He has never let me down, and I know in my gut he never will.

I climb back up on the horse, and Sage fans out my dress. I hear the click of the camera, but all I can focus on is getting to the church and not falling off the horse. Riding side saddle for photos isn't easy! How did those girls a hundred years ago do this?

The closer I get to the church, the calmer I feel and the bigger the smile on my face gets. As we get close, I hear the music and people talking, and it's just calming. We reach the tree line, and I see Dad in front of the church. He's in his element talking to people like he's known them their whole lives. I see the biggest smile on his face, one that has been missing the last few months.

When he spots me, his eyes widen, and that smile gets even bigger. As he makes his way over, the girls help me down from the horse, and a man I've seen around the ranch but never talked to before comes up and takes the horse back towards the barn. He must be a ranch hand. I should get to know them all a bit better.

"Baby girl, you look stunning. There just aren't words to describe how you looked up on that horse like that." I see Dad's eyes mist over.

"No tears, Daddy, not until after pictures!" I fake scold him, and he makes a big show of nodding and standing up straighter.

"Of course, after photos. Let's get you married to that amazing man of yours, shall we?" Daddy takes my hand and places it in the crook of his arm, leading me toward the church. I watch my bridesmaids all file in slowly one by one—Anna Mae, Megan, Riley, Sage, and Maggie.

We pause just outside the church door, and we both take a deep breath. Even without words, I'm fighting tears. I know what's going through Daddy's mind. These are the last few minutes I'm his little girl before he hands me off to marry the love of my life.

"I love you, Daddy, always."

"I love you too, Ella Bear," he says with his voice full of emotion.

Another deep breath and we start up the church steps. The music changes and I hear the shuffle of everyone standing up, but I don't see any of them as I enter the church. My eyes find Jason at the other end of the aisle, and nothing else seems to exist.

He's wearing what he calls his cowboy formal with his cowboy boots and khaki pants paired with his white button shirt and his brown sports jacket. He paired it with what he calls his dressy cowboy hat, and I've never seen a man look so downright sexy in my life. Suddenly, I can't wait for the wedding to be over with.

We slowly make our way down the aisle, and I watch Jason shift his weight from foot to foot then look down at the ground for a minute. When he looks back up at me, there's so much emotion on his face. I can see the tears in his eyes. He doesn't try to hide them. He just offers me a wobbly smile as he tries to not let them fall.

His tears trigger my own and in that moment, I give up on keeping my makeup in place. The girls will just have to fix it.

We make it to the front of the church, and I hear the pastor talk and my Dad, but I don't pay attention to a word they say. My eyes still haven't left Jason's. The next thing I know, I feel Dad placing my hand in Jason's, and I step into my place in front of the pastor. Not caring that all eyes are on us or what the proper protocol is, I reach up and gently wipe away the tears from the corner of Jason's eyes, causing him to smile at me.

"I love you, Ella," he whispers for just me to hear.

"I love you too, Jason," I whisper back, and we're lost in our own little bubble until the pastor clears his throat and earns a few chuckles from our family and friends.

We continue the service, say our vows, and exchange wedding rings. Then I get nervous again. I trust Jason, but my nerves get the best of me, and he can tell.

"Don't worry, sweetheart," Jason whispers to me just before the pastor speaks.

"I now pronounce you husband and wife. You may kiss the bride."

Jason leans in, and my heart races, and I can't breathe. His lips touch my forehead for a moment before he pulls back, and the whispers start in the church.

"Sorry, folks. Our first kiss isn't for public eyes," Jason addresses them, making me smile. Then he shocks the hell out of me and picks me up bridal style and caries me back down the aisle and out to his truck.

Once he has me settled in his truck, he races over to his side and climbs on in. Holding my hand, he drives down the driveaway toward his parents' house. He parks outside the barn. Before I even get the door all the way open, he's right there and takes my hand.

"Where are we going?" I ask.

He smiles. "Somewhere we can be alone for a few minutes. Come on."

He pulls me into the barn and into the barn office where he closes and locks the door behind us. I've been in here a few times, but I don't get time to take it all in this time. Jason is right in front of me again.

My heart races and judging by how hard he's breathing, his is too.

"Ella, Ella, Ella," he says as he lets out a breath he sounds like he has been holding.

"This dress looks amazing on you. You're so beautiful, so perfect, and so mine." Jason brings a hand up to my cheek and runs his thumb over my bottom lip before slowly moving his hand to the back of my neck. His other hand rests on my hip and pulls me forward toward him and slowly lowers his head toward mine.

His eyes search mine for any uncertainty, but he won't find any. I've never been so certain about something in my life, about him. I love this man so deeply. I can't wait for his lips to finally land on mine.

When the front of my body is plastered to his, and my head is tilts back, I look up at him. He slowly closes the space between us, painfully slow. It seems like hours tick by before finally, his lips are on mine.

His kiss is soft and sweet. His lips lightly dance over mine, sending tingles from every place they touch, straight to my core. I melt into him, and he deepens the kiss by pulling me closer to him.

His arm wraps around my lower back, holding me to him with no room left between us. I feel my nipples harden against the confines of my dress as my body sparks alive.

Jason lets out a low moan and spins us, so my back is against the door, causing me to gasp from surprise. He slips his tongue against mine. As he pins me to the door, I wrap my arms around his neck, trying to deepen the kiss. My whole body is on fire, and he's the only one who can put the fire out.

As he pins me to the door with his hips, his hands cup my face, angling it so he can reach my neck, and his kisses trail over my jaw to the spot just below my ear. When he lightly runs his teeth over the skin there, my body shivers. This time, it is I who moans.

His hand lightly traces a path down my neck and over my shoulders to gently cup my aching breasts, causing me to gasp again. As he's kissing the spot where my neck and shoulder meet, I rub my hands down his shoulders and down the front of his chest under his jacket, and I feel his body shudder. He attacks my lips again, this time pushing harder and deeper as his hand glides down and behind me to grab my ass. He almost lifts me off my feet.

I can feel his hard cock rubbing against my belly, and I want nothing more than to grab hold of it. My hands trail toward it and as if he knows my thoughts, his hands grip mine and pin them to the door above my head as he rests his forehead on mine.

"I don't want to leave this room. I don't want to stop kissing you, and I don't want you to take your hands off me. But your first time won't be here like this and if we keep going, I won't be able to stop."

I'm still trying to catch my breath, so I just nod. As he pulls his head back, his eyes meet mine. "That was one hell of a first kiss, Ella. I knew it would be good between us. I just never dreamed it could be this good."

"Me either," I whisper.

He lets go of my hands, and I let them fall to his shoulders as he wraps his arms around me and buries his head in my neck. We stand there for several minutes, just holding each other, trying to recover from that earth-shattering kiss.

Before we head back to his truck to meet everyone for pictures, he helps me fix my hair and my makeup best we can. We leave that barn office with our arms around each other, laughing and just enjoying the moment.

Chapter 26

Jason

The sun sets as we're doing our wedding photos in front of the church. Photos where I don't have to keep my hands off my girl. Photos where I can hold Ella and sneak in kisses every chance I get.

Soon as the photos are over, I'm about to drag her back to my truck when Sage stops us.

"Hey, give us a ten-minute head start before you head to the reception, okay?" she says and winks at Ella.

I just nod and head to my truck and help Ella inside. Telling me to wait ten minutes with my girl inside my truck is like starting a race. How fast can I get her to my truck and get my hands on her?

Once I close her door, I race around to my side of the truck and start the truck. I take a deep breath and look over at Ella, my wife.

Then at the exact same moment, we lunge for each other. Our mouths collide, and sparks ignite straight to my cock. This reception is going to be cut short. I don't know how much longer I can wait to be inside her.

After a few minutes of a good hot and heavy make-out session, I pull back and catch my breath.

"I don't think I'll ever get enough of you," I whisper against her lips.

"Good because I won't get enough of you."

I kiss her again, but softly and slow this time. Exploring her lips, every curve, every line I want to memorize.

Pulling away from kissing her is one of the hardest things I've ever had to do, but she has a surprise for me, something she's worked hard on, and I want to see it. If it's important to her, it's important to me.

"Ready to head to our reception?" I pull back and readjust myself in my seat.

She nods and does the same.

"I can't wait to see your surprise."

That seems to catch her attention, and her eyes light up.

"I'm a simple girl but when I saw the reception for Sage and Megan, I knew what I wanted for us."

I take her hand in mine and slowly drive us over to the event barn.

"I can't wait to see it."

"Oh, park right there," she says as she's practically bouncing in her seat.

I park and come around to help her out.

"Come on, we have to go around to the other side." She takes my hand and pulls me around. I don't see anyone outside the barn, figuring they must all be inside. It's almost dark now, so I don't think much of it.

When we round the corner of the barn, I see the most breathtaking setup I've ever seen on the ranch. There's an area with a bunch of rustic wood tables all pushed together to make one long table that has to hold over fifty people. The table settings are done up in natural greens and browns with lots of items that reflect the ranch, like slices of wood from a tree trunk with our ranch brand on them.

So many flowers from Mom's garden are scattered around. The chairs are made from rustic wood in all different styles like they were found at different thrift or antique stores.

Even with all that, the table and décor aren't what take my breath away. Above the table, strung up like a tent, are thousands of twinkle lights that give the whole area a magical glow. My eyes roam over it all, taking it all in before I look over at Ella.

She has been watching me with the biggest smile on her face. "What do you think?"

I have no words for how perfect this is, so I wrap her in a hug and pull her toward me. I see the wedding photographer off to the side, getting photos with the tables and lights behind us.

"Ella, this is the most beautiful thing I've seen, next to you. It's perfect."

I hold her for a moment more before I hear the barn door open and footsteps.

"So, big brother, what do you think?" Sage asks.

"It's perfect." I keep my eyes on Ella.

"Damn right it is, now let's get this party started!"

Ella and I sit in the middle of the table, our family sits around us, and friends spread out, to eat and talk. Everyone is laughing and having a good time, and I can't seem to keep my hands off my bride. I want to drag her out of here, so we can be alone, but I want to show her off. Today is all about her. I'm just the lucky bastard who gets to be by her side.

Once we finish eating, Ella bounces from person to person, getting to know everyone from town and taking me along for the ride. She wins over everyone she talks to, and I know she'll fit right into the town.

A slow song starts up, and I tug on her hand to get her attention.

"Come dance with me." I try to lead her to the dance floor.

"I don't know, Jason."

"Sweetheart, we're married now. It's you and me, and we make our own rules." I lean down to whisper in her ear, "I want to dance with my wife pressed up against me, so she can feel what she's doing to me tonight."

She blushes but lets me lead her onto the dance floor. When we reach the center, I pull her in close, so close our bodies are touching, and there's no room between them.

"Are you having fun tonight, sweetheart?"

"Yeah, everyone I've met is so nice. To have this kind of support is a dream of mine. I think I'm going to be so happy living here."

"I'll make sure of it, but I want you to make me a promise."

"Anything."

I chuckle. "If at any point you aren't happy, tell me, and I'll do everything in my power to fix it. Can you promise me that, sweetheart?"

"I promise. But, Jason?"

"Yeah?"

"Same goes for you, promise me?"

"I promise, but my happiness depends on yours. If you're happy, healthy, and mine, then I'm over the moon." I bury my face into her neck and just take her in. The way her body fits next to mine, and the way she moves against me. Her scent is now ingrained in my body.

When the song is over, I pull away just enough to look into her eyes.

"I love you, Ella. Today starts a new chapter for us, and I can't tell you what it means to me that you get to be in all the rest of mine."

Her eyes water as she looks into mine. "I love you too, Jason," she whispers, her voice full of emotion.

Our little bubble is broken when I hear the clinking of glass. It takes me a minute to hear it and look up to see all my family and friends watching us around the dance floor, clinking their glasses for us to kiss.

"What are they doing?" Ella asks.

"It's a wedding tradition. They want us to kiss. I guess they're feeling gipped they didn't get to see our first kiss."

Her face blushes. "I'm glad no one saw that kiss."

"Me too. What do you think? Should we give them what they want?"

She looks around the room and smiles then nods.

I gently bring my hands up to her face and rub my thumbs over her cheekbones before I lean in ever so slowly. She places her hands on my hips, and it's just a simple move, but one we haven't been able to enjoy before now.

I lightly bring my lips to hers, and the room bursts into cheers. I can feel her smile against my lips. I deepen the kiss and let my tongue explore hers for just a moment before I pull away, placing a quick soft kiss on her lips.

"Ready to get out of here, sweetheart? Because I'm ready to have you all to myself."

"Yeah, I have one more surprise for you."

This causes me to groan. "All I need is you." My voice sounds raspy to my ears.

I take her hand and lead her towards the door.

As we pass Sage, I say, "We're heading out. Have fun."

She laughs. "I'm surprised you lasted this long, big brother. Have fun!"

I can still hear her laughing all the way to my truck.

Chapter 27

Ella

It would be a lie if I said I haven't thought about my wedding night because I have. In detail and even more so after last night in Jason's room. So when Jason suggests we head out, there's no way I'd say no.

Tonight, we're staying at one of the cabins on the ranch. We head out to the lake house tomorrow. Jason said he would take care of setting the cabin up for us, so I'm excited to see it. We drive a bit towards the back of the property.

"This cabin was my great-great-grandparents' first home. It was the first house on the property. If you like it, I was thinking we could fix it up and live here when we have kids." I can hear the nerves in his voice as he tries to make normal conversation.

"I can't wait to see it. There has to be so much history there."

"There is. Plus, it's a bit out of the way, so we'll have our privacy."

A minute later, we pull out of the tree cover to a large open area with a beautiful traditional white clapboard siding. It's two stories that look almost exactly like the Walton's house in the TV show with the large front porch and all.

"Oh Jason, it's beautiful!"

"I thought you might like it. It has four bedrooms, two and a half baths, and I know you can't see it now, but the backyard is fenced in. It's not in bad condition. We could move in now if you wanted, but I think it would be good to do some remodeling too. It's been kept up well from generation to generation."

He's rambling, a sign he's as nervous as I am. I lean over the center console and press my lips to his to redirect his train of thought. Just as he realizes I'm kissing him, I pull back, causing him to groan.

"Let's head inside." I smile against his lips.

We head inside, and the house I'm sure is nice enough, but I don't register much other than we walk into the living room.

"The kitchen and dining room are back there and so is the master bedroom." Jason points toward the back of the house. "I'm going to set our bags down back there."

I watch him walk toward the back bedroom, and I slowly make my way to the area between the living room and dining room. When Jason comes back, he stops and leans against the doorway, watching me.

I take a deep breath and turn my back toward Jason.

Looking over my shoulder, I ask, "Help me out of this dress?"

I hear him take in a sharp breath before he walks toward me. When he's right behind me, he stops but doesn't touch me. I can feel his body heat radiating off him, and my body craves it, craves more. He brings his hands up and rests them on my arms just above my elbow and then slowly traces them to my shoulder as he leans in to trail slow soft kisses down my neck.

When his hands reach my shoulders, they move to the top of the dress to release the buttons on the lace. His lips never leave my neck. I tilt my head to give him better access and can't help the moan that leaves my throat at the feel of not just his hands on me, but his mouth too.

As his hands finish the buttons on the lace and move to the zipper on my dress, his lips move across my shoulder to my spine. As he slowly pulls the zipper down, his mouth is there to kiss the newly exposed skin until he reaches the back of my baby doll. He continues to slowly drag the zipper down as he torments us both. I hold the front of the dress so when he stops, and I turn around, it's still in place.

I can see the heat and need in his eyes, and his cock is rock hard behind his zipper. He isn't even trying to hide it. He looks me over and as he waits for me to let go of the dress, his breathing picks up and so does mine. Neither of us says a word.

I take a deep breath, steel my nerves, and let the dress fall to the ground. I swear for a brief minute Jason stops breathing, and his eyes widen as he takes in the sheer white baby doll and white lace thong I have on. Then he lets out a groan and reaches toward me.

"Holy shit, you had that on under the dress the whole day?"

I nod.

"Damn, sweetheart, good thing I didn't know. We wouldn't have even made it to the reception." I can't help but laugh, which quickly turns to a moan as he runs his hands over my breasts. He runs his thumbs over the stiff peaks of my nipples, causing me to gasp. No one has ever touched me like this, and every little movement has my nerves sizzling for me, and my barely there panties grow wetter. I squeeze my thighs together as I feel my own wetness coat them.

His mouth lands on mine, and it overwhelms my senses as his hands travel down to my waist. I grab onto his shoulders to steady myself, and his hands reach around to my ass.

"Wrap your legs around me, sweetheart," he says as he lifts me. I do as he asks, and he moves to the dining room table and sets me down again. His mouth never leaves mine and he lays me down on the table and lies over me. My legs still wrapped around him, I feel his hard cock press against my clit, and it causes me to gasp. He thrusts his hips forward, hitting my clit again. It's never felt like this, even when I would touch myself at night. Even after sneaking into Jason's room last night, it wasn't like this.

His hand trails from my hip down to the top of my lace panties, and he hesitates for only a brief minute until he slides over them and presses down on my clit, causing me to cry out.

"Jason!"

"I've got you, sweetheart. Let me take care of you," he mumbles into my neck as he slowly kisses down the center of my chest. He pulls up the fabric of the baby doll, keeping his eyes on me. Ever so slowly, he takes it off me until I'm in nothing but the lace thong.

"You're wearing way too many clothes," I say as I look at him, and he smirks.

"That's an easy fix." He unbuttons his shirt, but I sit up and stop him. His hands fall to his side, and I take a page from his book as I slowly unbutton each button and kiss the newly exposed skin. I see the goosebumps prickle across his skin with every touch of my lips to it.

When I undo the last button, I run my hands back up over his abs and chest to his shoulders and push the shirt off him. It pools on the ground at his feet, and I have the clear, up close, and personal view of his abs, but I want a view like the one I had last night, so I unbuckle his belt.

As I unfasten his pants, I brush against his cock, and I hear the sharp intake of air, so I do it again. A ripple runs through his whole body.

When I have his pants open, he pulls them down and steps out of them, leaving him in nothing but his black boxer briefs.

I bite my lip as I look at the outline of his large cock. I reach out to touch it, but he grabs my hand first.

"Can I see it?" I ask shyly.

I watch as he swallows hard, then nods and releases my hand. I run the palm of my hand over his length and grab the top of his boxer briefs and pull them down. His cock springs out at me. Jason steps out of them and stands back up, waiting for me to make the next move.

I wrap my hand around him, and he's hard but smooth as silk. I don't know what I had expected but not that.

"Will you show me?" I whisper.

He wraps his hand around mine and squeezes it tighter than I thought would be comfortable and then pulls my hand up to the tip that's already wet with pre-cum and then slides it back down.

"Just like that," he groans, so I continue with the long, firm strokes as more pre-cum drips out. I have the need to taste it. I push him back a little and stand.

He gives me a questioning look then I sink to my knees, and his eyes go wide.

"No, Ella, you don't have to do this. Not tonight, not like this."

"I want to know what you taste like, and tonight is perfect. This is what I've been waiting for."

Before he can get another word out, I suck the tip of his cock into my mouth and lick the pre-cum off it. Moaning, I take as much of him in as I can.

"Oh, shit. Oh God, Ella, that feels so good. I'm already so close. I'm not going to last long, sweetheart." He reaches over to grab the table, and I work him in and out of my mouth. When he grabs my hair with one hand, I'm worried he's going to pull me off but when he doesn't, I moan at the tight grip.

"Oh fuck, I'm gonna come," he groans, and I take him to the back of my throat and feel his release coat it. I swallow it all down and when he stops, he looks down at me in wonder.

"Holy shit, Ella."

I smile. "Was it good?"

He looks up at the ceiling then back at me.

"Was it good? I lost my shit in under a minute. If I hadn't been on edge from seeing you naked already, it would have been embarrassing." He reaches down and pulls me back up on to the table.

"Lie down, sweetheart. It's your turn now." He pulls my thong off, and it joins the pile of clothes on the floor.

He falls to his knees and slides my ass to the edge of the table and pulls my legs open.

"So beautiful," he murmurs right before he takes one long lick, causing me to yell out his name.

"I love hearing you yell my name like that, sweetheart," he says before attacking my clit with his tongue. My hips jerk, and a tight coil pulls from my belly down to where his tongue is. He grabs my hips to hold them still as he keeps attacking my pussy.

Then he moves one hand so his thumb can circle my clit as his tongue moves down and slides inside me. A feeling so foreign yet perfect that it only takes a few strokes. I'm coming harder than I ever have in my life. My body locks up, and my thighs clam around Jason's head. Through it all, he doesn't stop his assault on my body, and my climax just rolls right into a second one before I even know it's happening. I can't catch my breath, and I pull at his hair, but I don't know if it's to get him to stop or keep going.

When my body relaxes, he kisses his way up my belly to my breasts and lightly licks and sucks on each one, burying his face in my neck.

"God, Ella, I don't even have words for how amazing you are. That was the most beautiful thing, the way you came on my tongue like that, giving me that gift." His voice is hoarse with emotion. He sits up to look at me. "I love you."

"I love you too, Jason. Now take me to the bedroom and make love to me."

Chapter 28

Jason

I waste no time as I pick up my Ella and carry her into the master bedroom and lay her down on the bed. With her blond hair spread out against the white sheet, she looks like an angel, just like I thought she was the first night.

I'm suddenly nervous. She just came on my tongue twice and had her mouth around my cock, but this... This is huge. I sit on the edge of the bed and look at her.

"I want you so bad, Ella, but I want you to know, we don't have to do this tonight. I don't care what tradition or anyone says. This is you and me. I want you to truly be ready, not just because you feel like you have to on our wedding night."

She sits up, stands on her knees on the bed, and wraps her arms around my neck before sinking back down to eye level.

"I want this, Jason. I want you. If I thought I could have convinced you last night, I wouldn't have left your room. We would have done this last night or even a month ago. I was ready then, with you. I love you, and I want to make love with you. And I want more of what just happened in the dining room." She smiles.

I laugh then meet her eyes and nod. "Lie down, sweetheart. Let me take care of you."

I just pulled two orgasms from her, but I want another. I want her as wet and as soft as she can be. The thought of hurting her grips my heart.

I pull her legs wide and lean down to suck on her clit again. She's so responsive. Just a few hard sucks and I can tell she's already on edge. I kiss my way back up her body and line my cock up at her entrance. I kiss her.

"I hate that this is going to hurt you, but will you trust me to make it good for you?"

She smiles and wraps her arms around my neck. "I trust you, Jason. Always."

Bracing my weight on one arm, I reach down, use my thumb to circle her clit again, and slowly slide inside her. Only one inch and she feels like heaven. I keep circling her clit and as her hips jerk, I slide in a little bit more until I feel her barrier. Her grip on my shoulder tightens, and I hold still as badly as I want to thrust forward. I keep circling her clit a little harder and when I feel her start to come, I thrust all the way inside her.

Her moan turns into a scream of pain or pleasure, I'm not sure, and I bury my face in her neck and hold still while her body adjusts to me. I whisper to her how much I love her, how amazing she feels, and how I'm going to make her feel just as good too. Slowly, I feel her body relax, and she lifts her hips.

"How do you feel, sweetheart?" I ask.

"So full," she moans.

I slide out just a little, and she gasps and digs her nails into my shoulder. Then I slide back in, making sure I'm grinding on her clit, and she moans. A few more slow thrusts and any sign of pain is gone, so I pull all the way out and thrust back in, causing her hips to buck. She feels like heaven. A warm, wet, tight heaven that's strangling my cock.

"God, you're so tight, so perfect. I'm not going to last," I grunt and lean down to work her clit again. I take her mouth in a hard kiss and bite her lip as I pull back, and her pussy clenches around me, causing me to leak come into her.

I keep thrusting and look down to where we're connected and see the trail of her virgin blood on my cock. It's almost too much to take. I need her to come now. I pinch her clit, and her hips buck, and I can't hold back.

I start to come, and I thrust all the way inside her, a primal need to get my seed in her to get her pregnant. I've taken her without a condom tonight, without a second thought. She's mine, and I need to mark her in all ways possible. My hot cum coats her insides, and I pinch her clit again. Her orgasm hits her hard. Her nails dig into my back, and the pain just makes me come even harder. I can't seem to stop coming, and I feel it leaking out of her and down her thighs onto the bed, but I can't stop.

When her body relaxes, so does mine. I collapse on top of her and try to catch my breath. I can feel her heart racing against my chest, and it's a soothing pounding that slows mine.

I lean up and give her a soft kiss. I pour everything into that kiss. How much I love her, how much the gift she gave me tonight means, how I can't believe she's mine. When the kiss breaks, I look down into her eyes that are looking back at me. My cock is still inside her, and I have no plans to move just yet.

"Is it always going to be like that?" She asks.

I smile "With the pain? No. But how explosive it was? I don't know. I've never felt anything like that before, but I think it's us, and I'll do everything in my power to make sure it's always like that."

"I don't know if my body can handle it being like that every time."

I can't help but laugh. "I don't know. I can feed you and bring you anything you need. Keep you in an orgasm coma in bed all day. Sounds perfect to me."

She laughs, and I know it's time to get her cleaned up. I slowly pull out of her, seeing the blood of her virginity on my cock is still hard. As much as I want to go again, I'm reminded she'll be sore, and I need to take care of her.

I head into the bathroom to clean up. I get a warm washcloth and a towel and head in to clean her up. I lay a towel down under her before I crawl back into bed with her.

I pull her into my arms, tuck her against my side, and pull the covers up over us to soak up her body heat. I feel at peace.

"This is what I've been dreaming about every night. Holding you in my arms as I fall asleep and waking up with you in the morning."

She snuggles in closer. "Me too. The sex was amazing, don't get me wrong, but this is perfect too."

"This is perfect," I agree.

As tired as I should be, I can't seem to fall asleep. Even after I feel her breathing even out. I'm relaxed and have my girl in my arms, but I don't want to waste a minute of this. I know I have every night for the rest of our lives to hold her, cuddle her, make love to her. I drift off that night with a smile on my face and my whole world in my arms.

Epilogue

Mac

I'm on the way to the lake house with the family, and I have the same bunch of nerves I get every time we head out this way. Jason and Ella have been out here for the last week on their honeymoon, and this week we join them to give Ella a full lake house family experience like Blaze did with Riley.

I'm riding with Sage and Colt out to the lake house now, and I'm watching the landscape of northern Texas fly by. Every year since I became part of the family, we've been coming up here twice a year. This is the highlight of my year, these trips, but no one knows that. My family, who has given me everything, doesn't know I have a secret I hide from them that circles around this very lake house.

I tune out Sage and Colt who are arguing over the radio *again*, and I think of the last week since Jason and Ella got married.

We heard from the sheriff on Seth, or whatever his real name turned out to be, that he didn't make bail this time. Also, that charges have come in that they can link him to two murders, four rapes, and two other disappearances of girls so far. Evidence is still coming in from Jacksonville, Chicago, Norfolk, and Detroit. The dirty judge that granted him bail back in Tennessee has also been disbarred and brought up on charges.

Jason has asked us to keep the gruesome details from Ella for right now and let her enjoy this time, and I happen to agree. She's safe, it's over, and she just needs to focus on her new life with us.

Ella's family stayed on the ranch and only headed home to Tennessee yesterday. There has been some talk of them moving here after everything that happened at the church back home. I know Royce would love the idea. He's always around Anna Mae, and I can see something there, but she seems standoffish about it. Not that I can blame the girl after she caught her ex-husband cheating the way she did.

I check my phone for the tenth time since we got in the car and still nothing outside the group family text message on everyone talking about the trip and the ride.

Before I know it, we're pulling into the lake house just behind Blaze and Riley, who have Hunter and Megan ride with them. Mom and Dad pull in behind us, and all the noise draws out Ella and Jason. Jason seems to have a permanent smile on his face, and I can't say I blame him. He found his one. His girl and she wanted him too and they got married and just spent the last week hidden away together. I'd have a huge permanent smile on my face too if I were him. We all head up the walk, and Ella runs out to hug everyone.

"Come in, come in. We made lunch. Chicken salad sandwiches, coleslaw, chips, and brownies for dessert."

We all pile into the lake house Mom and Dad bought years ago. They bought it for just this day in mind, where our family would double in size and everyone would have their spouses here and later grandkids. Each couple has their own room, and there's a big walkout basement that's perfect for kids to camp out in. We can add bunk beds to later.

The food is set up buffet style, and I let the girls ahead of me, especially Riley with her being pregnant. She gets first dibs on the food. Megan and Hunter haven't said anything yet, but I have a feeling she's expecting too. I'm ready for that announcement anytime.

I watch Jason and Ella as I hang back and see Jason leaning his back against the counter and Ella leaning her back to his chest. His arms are wrapped around her, and they're both smiling and whispering to each other.

"It's such a nice day; let's eat on the deck," Mom says, so we all file out and grab our food and seats.

"So, what do you think of the lake?" I ask Ella.

"Oh, I love it here. The lake, the town, the people. It's a small town like Rock Springs, but the lake makes is so relaxing."

"It's a magical place for sure," I agree.

Ella looks at Jason and smiles. Jason nods, and Ella turns to Megan.

"Megan, are you still looking for someone at the shop?"

"I am." She looks at Ella.

"Well, Jason and I talked, and I want to go to cosmetology school."

"Oh! That would be perfect having my sister at the shop!"

They talk about school and what needs to be done as I lean back and take it all in. I can't help but feel something missing. *Someone* is missing. I glance at my phone and still nothing.

I look up when Mom sits beside me.

"It's great being out here with family, isn't it?" she says.

"Yeah." I force a smile.

"Your turn will come and soon, I feel it."

"I hope."

"You already found her, didn't you?"

I look at Mom but don't say anything.

"It's a gut feeling I have as a mom. You don't have to tell me anything, but if she's it, fight for her. Don't back down, don't let her friend zone you like Megan tried to do with Hunter. Push. Then next summer, you could be here with her. Our family will be complete as we add more grandbabies."

She pats my knee and stands just as my phone pings, letting me know I have a new text.

Sarah: Sorry. I'm working a shift at the diner, and we just finished our lunch rush. I hope you made it into town okay!

What the hell is she working at the diner for? She busted her ass to get her degree, and she's working at some small-town diner?

No way. I look around. Mom is right. It's time to get my girl.

• • • • • • • • • •

Want more Jason and Ella? Get a **FREE bonus epilogue in my newsletter here!**
https://www.kacirose.com/SweetheartBonus

Get Mac and Sarah's story in **The Cowboy and His Secret**

More Books by Kaci M. Rose

Rock Springs Texas Series

The Cowboy and His Runaway – Blaze and Riley

The Cowboy and His Best Friend – Sage and Colt

The Cowboy and His Obsession – Megan and Hunter

The Cowboy and His Sweetheart – Jason and Ella

The Cowboy and His Secret – Mac and Sarah

Rock Springs Weddings Novella

Rock Springs Box Set 1-5 + Bonus Content

Cowboys of Rock Springs

The Cowboy and His Mistletoe Kiss – Lilly and Mike

The Cowboy and His Valentine – Maggie and Nick

The Cowboy and His Vegas Wedding –
Royce and Anna
The Cowboy and His Angel – Abby and
Greg
The Cowboy and His Christmas Rockstar –
Savannah and Ford
The Cowboy and His Billionaire – Brice and
Kayla

Connect with Kaci M. Rose

Kaci M. Rose writes steamy small town cowboys. She also writes under Kaci Rose and there she writes wounded military heroes, giant mountain men, sexy rock stars, and even more there. Connect with her below!

Website
Facebook
Kaci Rose Reader's Facebook Group
Goodreads
Book Bub
Join Kaci M. Rose's VIP List (Newsletter)

About Kaci M Rose

Kaci M Rose writes cowboy, hot and steamy cowboys set in all town anywhere you can find a cowboy.

She enjoys horseback riding and attending a rodeo where is always looking for inspiration.

Kaci grew on a small farm/ranch in Florida where they raised cattle and an orange grove. She learned to ride a four-wheeler instead of a bike (and to this day still can't ride a bike) and was driving a tractor before she could drive a car.

Kaci prefers the country to the city to this day and is working to buy her own slice of land in the next year or two!

Kaci M Rose is the Cowboy Romance alter ego of Author Kaci Rose.

See all of Kaci Rose's Books here.

Please Leave a Review!

I love to hear from my readers! Please **head over to your favorite store and leave a review** of what you thought of this book!

Made in the USA
Columbia, SC
23 September 2024

42919063R00162